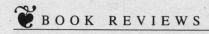

BOOK REVIEWS

Here's what people are saying:

. . . and the lightly humorous tone of the writing adds vivacity and appeal to the story.

from CENTER FOR CHILDREN'S BOOKS

. . . the episodes, told in first-person narrative, are warmly recounted, the writing is smooth, and Jessica is a solid, likable character to whom readers can easily relate.

from BOOKLIST

ALSO BY CORINNE GERSON

Son for a Day

FROM OTHER PUBLISHERS

Tread Softly
Passing Through
The Closed Circle
Like a Sister

Especially for Girls® Presents

How I Put
My Mom
Through
College

Original title: How I Put My Mother Through College

by Corinne Gerson

Atheneum 1982 New York

This book is a presentation of **Especially for Girls**®,
Newfield Publications, Inc. Newfield Publications
offers book clubs for children from preschool through
high school. For further information write to:
Newfield Publications, Inc., 4343 Equity Drive,
Columbus, Ohio 43228.

Published by arrangement with Corinne Gerson.
Originally published by Atheneum Publishers, an
imprint of Macmillan Publishing Company.
Especially for Girls and Newfield Publications are
federally registered trademarks of
Newfield Publications, Inc.
Printed in the United States of America.

LIBRARY OF CONGRESS CATALOGING-IN-PUBLICATION DATA

Gerson, Corinne.
How I put my mother through college.

SUMMARY: When Jess's newly divorced mother decides to
go back to college, Jess, in a reversal of rolls, listens to her
ideas and advises her on her problems.
[1. Mothers and daughters—Fiction. 2. Single-parent family—Fiction] I. Title. PZ7.G322Ho [Fic] 80-21681
ISBN 0-689-30810-8

Designed by M. M. Ahern

With love to Risa:
daughter
mentor
mentee
friend

How I Put
My Mom
Through
College

1

I'll never forget the exact moment Mom told me and my brother her big news. We were sitting under the cherry tree in our back yard playing Clue when we heard her car scrunching to a quick stop on the driveway gravel, then the doors slamming in the house. First the front door, then the back, and she flew out of it calling, "Jess, Ben, I was looking all over for you!" She swooped down on us, and Ben and I looked at each other with the same question on our faces: What's got into her *now?* But before we could ask she was answering:

"You'll never guess what I just did. I *registered.* I'm going to college!"

Ben's eyes bugged out and my mouth dropped open, but neither of us could say a word. After the worst summer of our lives, with Mom mostly staying in her room crying and Nana and Gramps coming over a lot to take us places and keep us distracted, this was a pretty big change. It must have been the first time Mom had smiled since she and Daddy had split up that spring. And I couldn't believe she really meant it about college because she hadn't done anything much more constructive than brush her teeth since then.

Ben jumped up. "You can't go to college! Who's going to take care of *us?*"

Mom blinked in surprise. "What do you mean? Why, I will, of course, the way I always—"

"How can you," he demanded, close to tears, "if you only come on weekends, like Daddy?"

She was down on her knees, laughing and hugging Ben close. "Oh, no, darling, not like that! I'm staying here with you. The college is only a half-hour away. I'll leave every morning and come back every afternoon, the way you do."

Ben got all excited and started jumping. "You mean you're going on the school bus with us?"

"No, I'll drive our car, but it will be the same kind of thing."

I was coming out of shock. "Are you sure you're going to like that, Mom? College is hard. Remember Frank?" He's her cousin, who flunked out his first year. "How do you know you're going to be able to study now that you're old?"

4

She burst out laughing, and I couldn't believe how beautiful that sounded. Ben was smiling now, and so was I. Anything was worth trying if it made Mom act so happy, even this crazy idea. "What do you mean *old?*" she cried, pulling me to my feet and twirling me around. "I'm only thirty-two! I know that sounds ancient to you, but nowadays lots of women my age haven't even had children yet. So I'm just a little ahead of the game."

"Did those women go to college when they were young?" Ben asked. He always asked dumb questions, but then he was only nine.

Mom laughed again. It was getting to be a regular comedy act. "Some did and some didn't. I guess you could say I'm just doing my life a little backwards."

Well, that turned out to be the understatement of the century. Because from that day on, not only was her life turned around backwards, but ours was, too.

Mom was so excited she cooked dinner that night. Mostly, since "The Crisis," we had had cold stuff or TV dinners at Nana's and Gramps's. Sometimes Ben and I had made spaghetti or franks and beans. That's another reason I'll never forget that day. Mom made stuffed chicken breasts and sweet potato pie. She even used wine in the stuffing, the way she did before "The Crisis"; and instead of making faces and pushing his plate away, Ben had seconds. It was the closest we had come to a celebration in longer than I could remember, and seeing Mom look so happy just about made me feel like a different person. When I look back at that time, I often wonder how I'd have felt if I'd known I would *become* a different person. You see, what really happened to me after that was that I, Jessica Amy Cromwell, at the tender age of thirteen, became a mother.

Oh, don't get me wrong—I didn't have a baby: I had a mother. A thirty-two-year-old mother who had just discovered she had to find out who she was. Had to "find her place in her life, in the world." Ben and I had always just assumed her place was in our house and our lives, doing all the things normal mothers do, the way she'd done all our lives. But times were changing, and we should have known it was too good to be true to have a father who came home from work every night and a mother who provided us with good meals and clean clothes and rides to our after-school activities. When Daddy first moved out of our house into his own apartment in New York, it was almost fun, because he came and took us out on weekends, and we saw more of him than we ever had when he lived at home. And everyone made such a big fuss over us you'd think it was me and Ben who were getting separated. But the fun part wore off pretty fast and things got awfully gloomy around our house. There wasn't any clean laundry around for a while, till Ben and I started doing it, or much in the way of real meals, and certainly nothing resembling family fun except when we were living it up with Nana and Gramps.

But even that got boring—getting spoiled all the time. Once in a while is terrific, but a steady diet was too rich for our blood. Ben especially. He began turning into a regular spoiled brat. The day I told that to Nana and Gramps they looked at each other and shook their heads and said, "Out of the mouths of babes." That was only a week before Mom came home with her big announcement.

Mom had spent a lot of time by herself after Daddy moved out, then she went to a counseling group and kept talking to all kinds of people, looking for something to sort of grab onto, and then she started collecting information about job skills and all that. She had married Daddy right after high school and had had me the next year and was just a mother and housewife all her life, so she had never been into any of that job stuff. Daddy had been in the Air Force and got a good job afterwards. He kept getting promoted, and by the time Ben was born they bought our house out on Long Island. I was four, and I don't even remember much about our apartment in Queens before that. My whole life—and certainly Ben's—was always our house and Mom and Daddy, and Nana and Gramps living about a mile away. When Mom and Daddy decided to split up, it was like a balloon bursting and the pieces scattering all over, and you could never fit them back together. But, as you'll see, it took us a long time to figure that out.

Anyway, the very next day after Mom made her big announcement we went shopping for school shoes, the way we did every year in August, as if the stores weren't going to have any left by the next month. The shoe places were always mobbed, and Ben always made a fuss about having to wait so long and Mom would keep asking the salesclerk if she was sure the shoes weren't too tight. By the time it was all over, we'd stagger away in relief, toting our new shoes and whatever dumb prize they were giving away that year and Mom would take us for banana splits to celebrate. But not this year. This time as soon as we got to the shoe department, Mom said, "Jess, you're old enough to take care of this. Let Ben pick out the kind he wants and make sure they fit, and the same for you. I need some shoes, too, so I might as well shop upstairs at the same time." She shoved a wad of bills into my hand. "Here, this should be plenty for both pairs. I'll meet you back here when I'm finished."

That's the first time I started feeling like a mother, but I was pretty used to taking care of Ben so it wasn't so strange. It was later, right after I got finished paying for Ben's and my shoes and Mom came rushing over to us and said, "Oh, I'm so glad you're ready. I want you to come up and help me decide which ones to take," that it started feeling odd. Luckily, Ben met his friend David, who had come with his mother for school shoes, and he invited Ben to go back home with them.

There was a whole mess of shoes and boots spread out all around where Mom had been sitting, and this skinny man with a fake smile was saying,

"Well, now you can consult with your fashion expert." Mom started trying all of them on and asking me which ones I liked best on her. "I need so much stuff," she was saying, "and I'm not going to have time to shop once school starts. Besides, these boots are on sale, so I'd be crazy to pass up the chance. Tell me which you like best, Jess."

It was a hot day and she looked awfully funny in her flowered sundress with the dark, heavy boots. "I don't know," I said, "it's hard to tell. They don't go with your outfit, Mom." And then, I couldn't help it —I suddenly remembered the day when I was eight and Mom and Ben picked me up after Susie Jasper's birthday party to shop for Ben's cowboy boots. I was wearing my yellow ruffly party dress and Mary Janes, and when the man brought the boots for Ben to try on I begged to try a pair, too. When I walked around in those clunky cowboy boots, all fancied up with white leather cutouts, everyone cracked up. Now, with Mom parading around in her flimsy sundress and heavy leather boots, it was like the tables were turned.

She was laughing. "I don't expect to wear them with this dress, silly. As a matter of fact, that's another thing I'd like to shop for today. Jeans. It's a perfect opportunity, we don't have Ben along to pester. Jess, feel the toes and see if they fit all right. Should I get them or the tan ones?"

The toes felt okay and I said I liked them better, so she bought them. And she took the clogs I chose, too. And the jeans, in the misses' department on the fourth floor, and two plaid shirts that I picked out.

"Daddy will have a fit when he sees the bills," she said when the clerk rang it up. "But I won't need much more clothing for the whole winter."

"Should I put it all in one bag," the clerk asked, "or do you want two so your sister can help carry part?"

I often wondered if that was what did it. That night—that very same night—Mom paraded around the house in her new plaid shirt and her new jeans that were as stiff as a board so that she couldn't even sit down and her new boots that were so hard she couldn't bend her legs. Her hair, which she had always worn up, was down now, flowing gorgeously over the back of her plaid shirt, and her eyes sparkled with pleasure as she posed for Nana and Gramps. Gramps kept shaking his head and saying, "Well, I don't know, going to college is one thing, but do you have to become a *teenager*?"

Nana was frowning. "I wonder, Ann dear, those jeans look awfully stiff. Aren't they terribly uncomfortable?"

"Oh, they'll loosen up, don't worry." She glanced at me. "Right, Jess?"

"Yeah, Mom, yeah. Listen, why don't you soak them in fabric softener for a couple of days. That'll get the stiffness out."

"Oh, that's right! That's what you do with yours, isn't it. I forgot all about it. Thanks, Jess. Uh—

what about the boots? How do you soften them up?"

I shrugged. "I don't know. Wear them a lot, I guess."

She did. She wore them around the house with her shorts for a few days while she went buzzing around being the happy little housewife that she hadn't been for a long time. Ben was so glad to see her that way he even helped, and the three of us started tearing the house apart, cleaning and polishing and scrubbing till everything sparkled. And all the time Mom kept saying, "We have to get it done now because we won't have time when school starts."

That was like a magic phrase for all of us, because we each had our own brand of excitement for what was going to happen in just a couple more weeks. Ben would be in fourth grade and have more than one teacher for the first time in his life. I was in seventh, starting junior high and scared and excited out of my mind. And of course Mom was starting college. The awful part of that year was finally over, and the good part was beginning at last.

Aunt Betty and Uncle Stan had a big family barbecue on Labor Day, and we had so much fun we didn't want it to end. There was a scavenger hunt for the kids, and the grownups sang old songs, and everyone made a big fuss about Mom and said she looked like Joanie's twin. Joanie was Uncle Stan's cousin. She was about twenty and in college, and she had the same build and coloring as Mom, small with golden-brown long hair. It was all sort of weird, because I started seeing Mom that way, too, like a young college girl. And it was not only the way she started looking, but the way she started *being*.

That very night she tiptoed into my room after I was in bed. "Jess, are you awake?" she whispered. I could tell she was all excited and wanted to talk, but I was too nervous about the next day myself and didn't feel like it, so I pretended I was asleep. But after that I didn't get off so easily.

2

The first day of school, our dinner table was like a talkathon. Everyone was jabbering away—everyone but me. I hated junior high, and I was still scared to death. Hardly any kids from Stevenson were in my classes; the teachers were too strict; and I kept getting lost changing classes. I had met some kids I knew at lunch and sat with them, but they didn't talk to me very much, they were so busy talking to each other. It turned out my friends from Stevenson had a different lunch period, so I decided to try to get mine changed to theirs. I went to the office and there was a big mob of kids waiting. The assistant principal announced, "If you're here to change your lunch period, forget it. No changes of schedules except for medical reasons." There was a mass groan, and practically everyone turned to leave, but I was determined.

"I'm diabetic," I told the assistant principal, vowing never to eat candy or cake again if they changed my lunch period.

He gave me a sympathetic nod. "I'm afraid you'll have to bring a note from your doctor. See me first thing tomorrow morning." I slunk away, hoping he'd forget.

Ben was all excited about trying out for the soccer team, and Mom was all excited about every single course she was taking. "I can't imagine how I'm going to keep up with all that reading. And doing the papers. Well, like I told you kids, you'll have to keep pitching in. We'll just keep up with our teamwork, and it'll all be cool."

I stared at her. So did Ben.

"What's the matter?" she asked. "Did I say something wrong?"

"Mothers don't talk like that," Ben mumbled.

"Like what?" she asked, her blue eyes wide.

I burst out laughing. "Oh, never mind. She can talk any way she wants, Ben."

"And they don't dress like that, either!" Ben growled, glaring at her.

She put an arm around his shoulder. "Now, Ben honey, you're just going to have to get used to it, because *this* mother *does*."

He shrugged, then smiled a little sheepishly. Mom winked at me, but I quickly started studying the food on my plate. This wasn't funny, and it wasn't fun. I had a mother and a little brother on my hands who were going to give me problems; I could just feel it in my bones. And I had enough problems of my own.

"Well, Jess, you haven't told us very much about how it went for you today," Mom was saying. "Did you meet a lot of new kids? Are any of your friends in your classes? You must be drowning in all kinds of things to tell us, and here we've been going on and not giving you a chance. Tell us, Jess."

I shrugged. "There's not much to tell. It's all so new. None of my friends from Stevenson are in my classes. They don't even have the same lunch period. I don't like any of my teachers all that much, not yet. And I keep getting lost."

"Wow, it sounds like junior high is really a hit with you!" Mom wasn't smiling now, but she didn't look worried, either, the way she used to whenever she thought something was bothering me. Then she did smile as she added, "Well, you'll see, one day everything will get turned around, I promise you. Oh, did I tell you about the student I met from India? She was wearing the most beautiful sari, and she was showing us how you drape it."

The phone interrupted, and I went for it. It was Daddy, wanting to know how our first day of school was. I said, "Fine, it was nice. I'm meeting lots of new kids and I like my teachers." I just didn't want to go through that again.

"Hey, that's really great, princess!" he said. "I was afraid it would be a little tough at the beginning, especially the first day. Well, leave it to you, you always fall into step. How about Ben? Put him on, honey; and when I see you this weekend, you can give me all the details."

While Ben was talking to him, I wondered if he was going to ask to talk to Mom to find out how her first day of school was. I don't know if he would have, because Mom called to Ben, "Let me talk to him before you hang up"; and when Ben gave her the phone she started telling Daddy about her classes and how much she knew she was going to like going to college.

My nine-year-old brother looked at me and said, "Doesn't it sound like she's one of the kids?"

That night when Mom came into my room after I was in bed, I just didn't have the heart to pretend I was asleep. She needed to talk and she certainly couldn't do it with Ben, so I listened as she told me how strange it felt for her to be among all these people so much younger than herself on the one hand and on the other hand how she didn't really feel cut off from them because she looked at things in the same way. The only difference, she explained to me, as if she were trying to convince herself, was that she had about ten years' more life experience. But the ideas and information college provided were all new to her in the same way they were to the others, so basically she didn't feel any different from the rest of them.

"I just hope they'll accept me, Jess. What do you think?"

"I don't know," I said.

She looked as if she were going to cry. "What do you mean—do you think they won't? Do you really think I'm too old?"

I sat up quickly and put my arm around her shoulder. "Oh, no, Mom, of course not! I know they'll accept you—why shouldn't they? You're just as smart as they are—probably smarter—and you have so much experience living out in the world and all, and you're so friendly and nice to be with, I'm absolutely positive you're going to fit in just like everyone else. You just have to give it a little time. After all, a person doesn't adjust to big changes overnight. Give yourself a few weeks and—and you'll probably be the most popular student on campus."

She giggled and hugged me. "Oh, Jess, I can always count on you for a super dose of self-confidence! Thank you, angel. What would I do without you?"

I don't think she even recognized her own words in there. She was too busy having her ego pumped up. And after all, it was the kind of thing she had done for me all my life. Now it was my turn.

My turn came every night. After she tucked Ben in, she would study for a while; and then, right after I'd go to bed, she'd come in for a "little talk." It would always start out with Mom asking me how things were going in school, and by the second day I learned just to say that everything was fine, and she'd sigh with relief and say she told me it would all work out and she certainly wanted to hear about my new friends. Then she'd start in on her day and the things she'd done and the people she'd met, and she'd keep asking me what I thought about everything—what people said to her and which groups she ought to join.

Every day I decided I was going to tell her what was happening in my life; but I just couldn't seem to get the words out. The way the little group of my friends from Stevenson huddled together, and each day another was sucked out into a new group of friends; it reminded me of a whirlpool, and every day I'd come to school wondering who was going to get sucked in that day, and if it would ever be me. The big problem was that Barb, my best friend all through Stevenson, had moved to Michigan right in the middle of sixth grade, and there I was, stuck without a best friend. Only a few months later Mom and Daddy had split up, so I hadn't been in any shape to find a replacement for Barb, not then or over the summer. But I'd figured I'd meet a lot of new kids once school started. Then when two weeks had gone by and I was as lonely and miserable as ever, I figured the smartest thing to do was to throw myself into the activity I seemed to be best at: being a mother.

Mom got piled up with so much schoolwork so

fast she had less and less time for the house, and that turned out to be the answer to my problems. I gradually took over most of the chores. It was something that got me through the day, something to hurry home for. I tried to get Ben to help me, but mostly he was out having fun, and when he was there he'd complain so much about anything I wanted him to do that it was easier just to do it myself. Laundry, fixing meals, cleaning—all the stuff mothers usually do. It started looking like I was being some kind of weird angelic type. I didn't tell anyone except my diary the real reason I was doing all this, and no one knew where the key was. Each day, as someone else from my old school group got caught in the new whirlpool, I took on an extra chore at home.

The trouble was, everyone started feeling guilty about it. Mom kept saying I didn't have to do it all, that we would all share, but you could tell she was really relieved to have this little elf around the house taking care of everything. And Ben kept telling me I didn't have to be such a big shot and that all I was doing was making him look bad. Then we'd get into a fight, and he'd clobber me with, "Besides, you're doing all the easy stuff, anyway, and when it comes to my turn, I'll have to do all the hard stuff." I never could get out of him what was the easy stuff and what was the hard stuff, but I figured he was just jealous because of the way Mom kept thanking me and telling me how wonderful I was. It just about saved my life, because when all the other kids were out after school doing all the new things they found so terrific, I could throw myself into cleaning and washing and cooking up a storm.

Even Daddy started getting on me about it when we'd see him on weekends. "Your mother tells me what a wonderful helper you are now that she's started college. That's very nice, Jess, but it sounds to me as if you're overdoing it a little. Ben, are you doing your share to help out?"

"Are you kidding?" Ben would screech. "Even if I wanted to, she wouldn't let me. She likes to do all the fun things, and she makes me be the slave and just carry the laundry up and down the steps."

I'd explain to Daddy then that I really didn't mind doing it and I had the time and Mom didn't, and Ben wouldn't be able to do half the things right anyway. Then Daddy would put up his hands to ward off Ben's argument about *that* and finally let it go.

Somewhere during all this time—I never knew just when—Mom became a new person. Not different, or changed, but *new*. One afternoon we were talking, and I looked up at her and she was standing there smiling at me; and I blinked because it didn't look like Mom any more, and it didn't sound like her, either, even though she had the same voice.

"It's really cool, Jess," she was saying. "I suddenly saw the whole thing through the perspective of three thousand years of history. The evolution of all that civilization, to end here, right here with people like you and me. *Us*. Products of all of that accumulation of wisdom and experience, and each of us making our own contribution in our own unique way. From our own personal space! Do you know what I mean, Jess? Do you get the cosmic significance of it?" Her blue eyes were wide with discovery, her golden-brown hair almost quivered from excitement as it lay in long silken strands over her plaid shirt, reaching almost to the top of her jeans.

I nodded my head uncertainly, not having the foggiest notion of what she was talking about. But she just kept blabbing on about fundamentalism and existentialism and a couple of other isms while I kept studying this new person standing in front of me. She was gesturing all over the place with the kind of excitement I wished I could muster for anything, even schoolwork.

That weekend she took Ben and me out to show us the campus. After the tour we had lunch in the dining hall, and Ben kept getting mad when Mom's friends came over and made a big fuss over us being her kids. Actually, it was Ben they made a fuss over. They didn't know exactly what to make of me, being so old. After all, I was almost thirteen and some of them were still in their teens themselves. A lot of them even had sisters and brothers my age. So they just kind of smiled at me and tried not to treat me like a little kid. But they didn't have that problem with Ben, and he hated every minute of it.

I watched as they clustered around him, Mom sitting there with one arm around his shoulder while she gestured with her other hand about something, and as I looked from one to the other, all the girls in plaid shirts or sweaters and jeans and long hair and boots, it struck me how they all looked alike. That's when I started playing a little game with myself. I closed my eyes for a split second, turned my head to a different spot each time, then opened them and turned around real fast and counted to see how many counts it took me to pick out Mom. I did it four times. It took eight, six, four, and two. But that eight was what got to me.

"Hey Mom, remember when I went to pick up Ben from kindergarten that first time it rained?" I asked her later. She had been telling me about her philosophy class, and something she said reminded me of it.

She paused a moment to think. "Not really, no. Did something special happen? You were always such a little mother! But what does it have to do with Schopenhauer?"

I laughed. "Nothing. I just remembered, though: Ben was wearing his yellow rain slicker and all the other little boys were, too, with those funny yellow head things, and I couldn't tell which one was Ben, not till he called to me. They all looked exactly alike!"

She grinned. "Oh, yes, I remember that happening to me, too! I'd always think, 'I ought to put some colored tape on his sleeve,' but I never remembered to. Anyway, we always found each other, so it didn't matter. Whatever made you think of that, anyway? Oh, *I* know—because I was talking about individuality, and being one's own person. That's what Thelonius was telling me. He was saying he's been watching me emerge from my cocoon, the gradual process of how I'm becoming my own person."

"Who's Thelonius?" I said absently. But I was thinking about how Mom had become one of those people in the yellow slickers. How she had become the College Student She Never Was, and though the uniform and the new language didn't turn her into that by itself, it sure tied up the whole package.

"—and blond and just gorgeous, Jess. He's a real Greek god!" She had this silly grin, and I didn't know who she was talking about for a moment. Then I remembered.

"He's a philosophy student. A dropback."

"A drop*what?*"

"You know—he was out of college for a while, being a carpenter, doing environmental studies, all that. Now he's back to get his degree. He's majoring in philosophy. Isn't that perfect?"

"For what? Is he going to be a carpenter again after he graduates?"

Her laugh was the trill of a teenager being tickled. "Oh, Jess, you're so funny sometimes. And so *true!*"

"Well, I didn't mean to be," I said, shrugging. "What do you mean, *true?*"

She hugged me. "Real. Authentic. You get right

23

to the heart of things. Listen . . ." She stood back, put her hands on my shoulders and looked into my eyes very, very seriously. "Thelonius wants me to—well, you know—go out with him."

"What's wrong with that? You told me you and Daddy were going to go out with other people, and . . ."

She sighed. "I know, but I think this is really it, Jess. I've never known anyone like Thelonius. He's like—well, in a way he's like you. Direct, simple, smart, and *true*."

"Well, I guess it's better than being false," I mumbled, trying to be funny because I couldn't think of a single other thing to say. I mean, what do you do when your mother asks you whether you think she ought to go out with a guy? The next thing you knew she'd be asking me how late she could stay out.

". . . and I hope you'll feel comfortable about it, Jess, but after all, you're practically thirteen."

"About what? Your going out with Thelonius?"

"Oh, no. I mean about staying alone a lot. You and Ben. I mean—how late do you think I can stay out?"

3

Well, that's the way it went. Actually, Thelonius was pretty interesting. And Mom was right, he was a Greek god. I'd say he was about the best-looking of any of the guys Mom went with that whole first year. He was nice, too, but awfully quiet. He would come and sit around the house with us, but he'd hardly ever talk. Whenever he did, he was always very pleasant. But mostly Mom kept jabbering away at him about all her ideas and the things they studied together, and he'd just sit and listen and smile at her and ask a question or make a brief comment here and there. It only lasted a few months, though, because Thelonius couldn't stand college life and decided to go traveling and dropped out again. But by then Mom had gotten into this really tight circle of girls and guys who used to do everything together—study, party, have discussions till the middle of the night. They never just talked—they had dialogs. Some of the group lived in the dorms, some lived off campus the way Mom did, and they were all different ages, up to Barry who was forty-five and retired from the police force when he decided to start college. On weekends Mom would fuss with her hair and her makeup for hours before she went out; she had started using makeup that made you look as though you weren't wearing any. And she'd keep coming into my room to ask me how she looked or what went with what. Sometimes it would take her ten minutes to decide which knee socks to wear. She wore them with jeans, and you couldn't see them anyway, except for what showed through from her clogs or sandals; but the way she acted, you'd think she was joining a knee-sock contest.

But the clothes weren't anything compared to our sessions. That's how I always thought of them. She'd tiptoe into my pitch-black room in the middle of the night after she got home, turn on my dresser lamp, kneel down on the floor beside my bed, and whisper in my ear, "Jess, honey, are you awake?" I never knew how long it took before I woke up, but sometimes she would shake me ever so gently, and of course I knew she'd just keep at it till I said something. Then she'd sit on my bed cross-legged and start telling me about the whole night and what people said to her and what she said to them and ask what did I think someone meant when they did a certain thing. Most of it never made much sense to me. But I'd always think of some kind of answer, and she always went for it. She'd hug me and say things like: "That's why I love sharing like this with you, Jess. You're so wise and unfettered. I know it's silly to say to a daughter, but I tell everyone how I get my best guidance from you, believe it or not." And things like: "I guess you could almost say we're growing up through these difficult and changing years together, couldn't you?" Sometimes I'd just shrug because I didn't have a real answer, but that never seemed to matter to her; it seemed to be more important for her to ask questions sometimes than to get answers to them.

Of course, she did some serious studying, too. Oh, boy, did she study! She did a lot in the library between classes and then for a few hours every evening after dinner. Usually that was the time Ben and I did our schoolwork, too, so it was always nice and peaceful in the house. Well, of course, Ben didn't have much to do, so he filled in his time watching the TV programs we had all decided it would be okay for him to watch. That included Daddy, too, because that was one of the things he and Mom had fought about a lot when they were together—that she let us watch too much TV. Ben kicked and screamed at first when we cut out some of his favorite programs. The ones with a lot of fighting and gore. He would beg and plead with Mom, but I would keep staring at her so she'd remember her promise to Dad, and she held up. When Ben and I saw Daddy on weekends, Ben started making jokes about it; and in a while he had replaced the bad favorites with some other good ones, and everyone was happy.

Daddy always asked me about everything we did, and I had a harder time getting past him with my problems than I did Mom. He didn't really make me say it, but I had the feeling he understood what was happening. He'd say things like: "Don't forget, you're in a whole new situation now and it takes a while to get used to everything being so different. Give yourself time, sweetie-pie." I'd feel like crying then and telling him I'd never get used to it, that I hated the way our new life was, with just having a father on weekends and not really having a mother at all. Not having any friends and hating school. But I didn't dare say that to him, because Ben kept saying things like that and making him feel rotten. So I said it to my diary instead.

I met Elly the day Mom had to drop biology. I was so embarrassed. That day in English Mrs. Jurgens announced that the school paper needed reporters and anyone was welcome to join. As I was leaving class, she touched my arm. "Jessica, why don't you come after school? You write very well; we could use someone like you." Why not? I thought as I hurried off to history. At least I'd be expanding my horizons.

So I went. The room was all noisy with kids sitting around in groups, or sitting by themselves at desks looking lost, or wandering around trying not to look lost. Mrs. Jurgens was over in the corner with three boys who were arguing about something. I just sat at a desk on the side and started looking around. Before I got too far, I was staring into a pair of huge, almost-black eyes. "Hi," came a crackly voice, one that sounded as if it was trying to keep from laughing. "Are you new, too?"

I nodded, wondering why I couldn't have coal-black hair like that instead of mousy brown. "I have Mrs. Jurgens for English, and she asked me to come to work on the paper."

"Me, too. My name's Elly Romanov. What's yours?"

"Jessica Cromwell, but everyone calls me Jess."

"Hi, Jess. My real name's Eleanora, but no one calls me that but my mother. She thinks it's a sin to spoil beautiful names. Do you like to write? I love to. I'm going to be a poet. Or maybe a journalist. I want to go out for photography, too. Do you belong to any clubs?"

She kept smiling at me while she was talking in her nonstop way, and something inside my chest suddenly felt as if it had been loosened from an ice block and was warming and floating away. "Yes," I said. "I mean, yes, I like to write, and no, I don't belong to any clubs. Let's see, did you ask me anything else?"

She was giggling now, and it sounded like ice

cubes bouncing off of rocks. "I'm sorry, Jess, I do run off at the mouth. I guess it's because I come from such a big family! I'm afraid I won't get it all in if I don't hurry."

Mrs. Jurgens started the meeting and talked about the different kinds of things we could do on the school paper, and then she asked us to sign up on the assignment sheet. Elly signed up before me, and by the time I got to it, she was gone. I was disappointed and hoped I'd see her again when we worked on the paper. As I left the room, a hand grabbed my arm.

"What took you so long?" Elly was standing just outside the door. "Where do you live? Want to come to my house?"

We lived four blocks apart, but she had gone to parochial school and I to public. We decided to go to my house because I thought I'd better check on Ben; and right after she phoned her mother to tell her where she was, Mom burst into the house. She was so upset she didn't even see Elly at first and started wailing, "Oh, Jessie, I had the most terrible battle with Professor Newman today! She's so cruel and heartless. I've been trying so hard in biology; but instead of giving me credit for my efforts, she's been really bearing down on me and making my life miserable. Just because I was wincing and gagging when we had to dissect that parasitic worm, she bawled me out; and then after class she told me either I had to drop biology or she's going to flunk me." She laid her head on the kitchen table and started heaving all over with sobs, and Elly's big, dark eyes got even bigger.

"Oh, Mom, it'll be okay. You'll be better off if you don't have to take biology anyway, you've been having such a hard time with it."

She looked up, her face tear-streaked like a little kid's. "I know, but I have to take a science credit, and it's too late to take another science this semester. Oh," and she suddenly noticed Elly. "I'm sorry, I never even realized anyone else was here!" She started laughing and wiping off her face as I quickly introduced them. "You have to forgive me, Elly," she said nervously, "but I get carried away. You see, it's my first year, and I take everything so seriously. I guess I just needed to let off some steam. Jess is awfully good for that."

"Gol-*lee*," Elly said afterwards when Mom went up to shower and we each had a doughnut, "I never dreamed you'd have a mother like that! That *anyone* would. She goes to *college*? She must have gotten married when she was a little kid. *Thirty-two?* Oh, come on, Jess. Really? That's how old Gilbert is."

Gilbert, I soon learned, was Elly's oldest brother. He was married and had an eight-year-old daughter. "Imagine, I'm an aunt!" she crowed. "Little old me! I got to be one when I was five. Hey, get this: my niece is about the same age as your brother!" There were four more brothers, all a lot older than Elly. Her mother was almost as old as my grandmother. "I was the toy," Elly explained. "You probably think I'm a spoiled brat. No such luck. My parents are real strict. Boy, it must be fun having a mother like yours. More like having a big sister. And a little brother, too. Some people have all the luck! Listen, I have to go now. Thanks for the jelly doughnuts, they're my favorite. Say good-by to your mom and Ben for me. And plan to come home with me after school tomorrow, okay?"

I wrote it in my diary that night, that last sentence. And after it:

I hope she doesn't forget. She seems very scatterbrained, so she might. But she's the most fun girl I've ever met in my whole life. She would be such good material for a best friend.

She didn't forget. And I was right. She was super material for a best friend.

4

I would say that the rest of that year was definitely up. First of all, because of Elly, I finally got sucked into the whirlpool. We started going to each other's houses after school and working on newspaper assignments together, and I never even knew when it was I realized I was spending more time with her than I ever had with Barb. By that winter Elly's house was my second home.

I was crazy about Elly's mother, too. She had Elly's black hair and dark, dancing big eyes; but where Elly was tiny, her mother was tall and large-boned. She was always cheerful and warm, and anything she said sounded charming with her slight foreign accent. Elly's father talked the same way, and he was nice, too, but he was a more quiet type. Even though Elly was the only one left at home, her brothers and their wives and kids were always coming and going, and the place constantly buzzed with activity. Mrs. Romanov did a lot of cooking and baking and sewing, and the house always smelled so good you could work up an appetite just walking through the front door. She'd always have something freshly baked and wonderful waiting for us after school, with mugs of hot chocolate when it was cold out, or icy glasses of milk when it got warm.

Sometimes I'd bring Ben there after school, and he loved having the goodies, but he'd always want to scoot right afterwards because Mrs. Romanov practically gobbled him up with motherliness, and he couldn't stand it. She was old-fashioned in a lot of ways, and I'm sure she thought it was terrible that my parents were split up and that my mother was going to college and leaving us kids alone a lot. Of course, she never said a word about it. She'd just get the feeling across by the way she tried to mother me and Ben. But I liked it, because she was so nice and loving and really cared about me.

Sometimes when we'd all sit around the kitchen table after school, she and Elly and Ben and I, and we'd be telling her about what happened at school that day and eating her scrumptious apple strudel, I'd wish I could bring Mom along so she could enjoy it, too. Then I'd have to laugh at myself, because I'd realize I was picturing Mom sitting at the table like one of the kids instead of like the other mother. But then, like I said before, that's the way it was going with Mom that year.

By the second semester, Elly and I had become very tight, and Mom's bumps started straightening out. She was taking chemistry for her science, and she was glad about it, because that's when she got all interested in nutrition. She thought she might even major in it.

Eventually Mom went on a natural-foods kick. Bulgar wheat and tahini and banning all junk foods. Oh, boy, she and Ben had some royal battles about that, and Daddy even got into the act a couple of times. He told her he didn't care if that's what she wanted to do, but that it wasn't fair to us to go whole hog like that without any warning. Then she'd say that where our health was concerned anything was fair, and wasn't her judgment better than a nine-year-old's. So he'd say he often wondered; and of course they'd be off again.

But that all got worked out, too. Actually, they hardly fought at all anymore. But of course they didn't have much chance to. And they even started telling each other about their social lives. By then Mom was going out with McKeever. That was his first name. McKeever Rudolph. He worked at the college and was a real grownup. Daddy was going out with a lawyer. She worked for Legal Aid and was divorced but didn't have any kids. I didn't like her all that much, but Ben really hated her. Daddy had taken us over to her apartment, supposedly because he had to drop off a briefcase she'd left in his car, but I think he staged the whole thing so we could meet and size each other up. Well, it didn't work out very well, because Daddy had to keep forcing conversation, and she tried to think of questions to ask us and only came up with dumb ones, and all Ben kept saying was, "When're we going to *go?*"

Afterwards Ben started giving Daddy the business about why he and Mom couldn't just patch up their "fight" and come back and live with us again, and Daddy started one of his eternal explanations, and Ben threw a tantrum, and Daddy finally lost his patience, and I started crying, so the whole day was a disaster. We were supposed to sleep over at his apartment and go to an antique car exhibit the next day, but Ben carried on so much that Daddy took us home instead.

I was mad at Ben because that was going to be the first time we'd slept over at Daddy's. He had a cute studio apartment in New York. It was on the twenty-sixth floor and had a terrace that looked out over the East River. We had brought our sleeping bags and were going to sleep out on the terrace, and we'd been looking forward to it all week. Ben pouted the whole half-hour drive out to our house on Long Island, and I didn't feel like talking, either, so Daddy just turned on the radio. Ben ran out of the car without even saying good-by, and Daddy looked as if he were going to cry himself. "I'll make it up to you, Jess honey. Ben is just taking this whole thing very hard."

"What about me?" I wrote in my diary that night. But the next day when Elly's parents invited me to go ice skating with them and I saw Ben go sulking off with Mom and McKeever for a bike ride, I realized it wasn't as hard on me. Especially since Elly and I had become best friends.

We had the sleepover at Daddy's the next weekend, and it was more fun! It was pretty cold out there on the terrace at night in the middle of March, but we wore warm pajamas and our sleeping bags were snug. Daddy gave us a little transistor radio to fall asleep with, and then a bright light woke me up. It was the sun, the next morning. I woke Ben up to show him how beautiful it was, all bright and clear on the river like that, with the little barges bobbing around down there and the different shapes and colors of the buildings on the other shore.

Daddy took us to a restaurant for a fancy brunch, and then we went to the antique car exhibit, so we really made up for the disaster of the weekend before. But Ben got sulky on the trip home again, and Daddy's mouth started tightening up. It was early, and Mom wasn't home yet. Daddy was annoyed. "She'll be home by ten," I told him. "She always is on Sundays, because she has an early class on Monday."

"Should I wait?" he said. When I laughed and told him not to be silly, that I was used to babysitting by now, he hugged me and looked relieved. Ben started grabbing him and not wanting to let go, and Daddy made it into a joke; but when he finally turned to go, I saw the unhappy look on his face.

We all got used to it, though, as time went by. Even Ben, but he had more ups and downs than anyone else. Meanwhile, Mom and McKeever broke up a few times and kept getting back together, until one spring afternoon she came home looking very funny. Before I could even ask her, she said, "Oh, Jess, I just had the most spiritual experience."

"Oh, no!" I groaned. I had read a long article about religious cults, and had a vision of Mom becoming a Hare Krishna and shaving off her hair and wearing orange curtains and disgusting rubber thongs. Leave it to her, she was ready for something like that.

"Oh, yes, and you'll never guess where."

"On Main Street?" That's the kind of place the cults often approached people, I'd heard.

She laughed. "No, silly. I went on a nature walk with the college Audubon Society. Randy from my British Poetry class invited me along. We went to a marsh near the campus, and it was a whole new world, Jess!"

I could only sigh with relief that she hadn't been snared into being a Moonie or a Hare Krishna. "Randy?" I repeated. "Is she the one who came for lunch that day?"

"It's a he. Randall Sweeney Armbruster. Isn't that a perfect name for a poet?"

"I guess so. If his poetry's any good." She tinkled

a happy laugh. *Oh-oh*, I thought. *This is the next one.* "Is he a dropback, too?"

"Not exactly He's more like me, never went to college till now. He's a freshman, too."

"Oh, that's good. I was afraid he was young."

"Well, he is, in years. I mean, he's only twenty-four, but he's *light* years older than I am in so many ways. He's traveled all around the world, worked at about everything in existence, and can do just about anything." The adoration in her face made me a little sick.

"Well, what does he need to go to college for?"

"That's what I asked him!" she cried. "But he said he wants to fill in the formal part of his background so he can be a more enriched person. He's coming over Saturday, and we're going to bake bread. He's a vegetarian, and he's going to bring copies of his special recipes."

I stopped listening. Instead, visions appeared of no more hamburgers, no more lamb chops. It was bad enough having to cut out bacon and hot dogs because of all the nitrites and stuff. Ben still got hysterical over *that*. But *now* . . . I groaned.

"Oh, I know you'll be crazy about him, Jess. I can't wait for you to meet him."

I didn't have to wait long. Saturday was in two days, and Ben and I were having seconds of Mom's homemade granola when the doorbell rang and she came back with this tall, skinny guy with funny red hair and a scraggly beard. He wore a rumpled tee shirt and worn jeans and sneakers and looked about

39

nineteen. Ben started choking on a raisin right after Mom introduced us, but they didn't notice right away because they were so busy talking. I yelled, "Mom, Ben's choking!" Randy rushed over, grabbed him from behind, locked his hands in a fist in the middle of Ben's chest and pulled in real hard, and the raisin came flying out of Ben's mouth. That was the only good thing Randy ever did for any of us.

He and Mom baked some whole wheat bread that day, and I must admit it was really good. But believe me, after that it was all downhill. After being the big hero, he rested on his laurels and started being a leech. He hung around all the time, eating up a storm, watching TV or playing rock albums real loud on the stereo. Ben couldn't stand the sight of him. Luckily, it only lasted a month, because then the semester was over and he took off for Florida to teach scuba diving for the summer. I was sure that was the end of it, that he wouldn't come back. But he did, just like the migrating birds.

He arrived the week before Mom's fall classes began. She had gone to summer session and took a whole bunch of courses, because by the end of her first year she was so into college she decided she was going to want to go to graduate school when she finished. That was my last summer as a camper at Harborside, a fantastic day camp that Ben and I had both gone to since we were seven. It's really what saved our summer that year. Harborside used to be a rich family's estate right on Long Island Sound. It's so beautiful, sometimes they use it as the setting for movies. In winter it's a private school, and in summer it's a day camp that Daddy's cousins run, so we get a big discount. At thirteen you get to be a senior camper, but after that you can't come back unless you get picked to be a junior counselor. But the seniors get to sail, and that's what made my summer. That and Elly going to Harborside, too. I saw more of her and her family that summer than I did of my own, because Elly's mother or brothers drove us and Ben back and forth. Mom had found a part-time job doing surveys for a market research company, so between that and her summer classes she was busy day and night. Ben and I kept the house running, me mostly; it had become second nature by then.

Daddy really appreciated Mom's helping out with a job, and they got real friendly. That's all Ben needed to start him on his old routine about their getting back together, so they each had to keep giving him these little talks. Especially now, because they had definitely decided on a divorce, and it was going to go through in a few months.

Actually, that came as sort of a shock to me. I didn't say as much as Ben, but when I saw the way they were getting along, I must admit I had had thoughts about their patching it up, too. After all, I thought, they'd both had a chance to get it out of their systems, and they ought to be ready for a fresh start. But when they told us about the divorce, and I saw how nice they were to each other, and polite and all, I suddenly understood that there wasn't any more going back for them. They had worked it all out, as they kept trying to explain to us; it was because that was all behind them that they were able to be different with each other. They could sort of stand off and be more like strangers with each other. I tried to explain it to Ben, but it was too hard.

It was the next fall, when Mom started her second year, that we found out about Margie. Right after Randy had come back and Mom had started seeing him constantly, I sensed that Daddy was going out with someone special. I knew it wasn't the lawyer, but I didn't know who it was. I had the feeling Ben sensed it, too, but we never talked about it. Maybe we both felt that if we ignored it, it would just go away. We still had our visiting day with Daddy every weekend, and he always planned fun things to do, so the routine had become comfortable. Then one day Daddy told us a good friend of his was coming along to the hockey game.

"Her name is Margie, and we've been going out for a while, so I want you both to meet her."

"Does she like hockey?" Ben asked.

"Yes, she loves it. But there's one problem. She's a Rangers fan."

Ben stopped dead. "Are you crazy?" he shrieked. "She can't come with us!"

Daddy swatted at him playfully. "That's what you think, buddy!"

Margie had blond, fluffy hair and a soft voice. She laughed a lot and talked pretty much, too. She was very nice, and very young.

It was kind of funny, the three of us screaming away for the Islanders, our team, and Margie rooting for the Rangers. The first two times the Rangers scored, Ben glared at her furiously; but then when our team scored and Ben started jumping up and down and yelling, she giggled and grabbed him and hugged him, and after that he kind of warmed up to her. Once, when two of the players were fighting real hard over a bodycheck, she looked over at me. "You don't like this part either, do you, Jess?"

I shook my head. "I know it's supposed to be part of the show, but I always hate it."

She squeezed my hand. "Me too."

"Aw, you're just sissies!" Ben said, and he and Daddy exchanged knowing looks.

"Oh, no we're not," Margie snapped. "We're pacifists. Right, Jess?"

I grinned at her. "Right, Margie."

Our team won, 4-3. Margie smiled and shrugged. "The best man can't win every time," she said, winking at Ben.

He grinned back at her. "Oh yes, they can, and they just did." He could afford to be bighearted now; and when we went for ice cream sodas afterwards, we were all talking and laughing together like old friends. I didn't remember when I'd seen Daddy look so happy.

After we got home Mom wanted to hear all about Margie. It was funny, because Daddy never made a fuss about Mom's boyfriends. For that matter, we never took them seriously, either, Ben and I. Not till Randy came along and Ben had this awful hatred for him. I wasn't crazy about him myself, but he just didn't bother me the way he did Ben.

Anyway, I figured it was an especially bad time for Ben because of the divorce. It came through just about the time we met Margie. Mom and Daddy had explained it so many times, and told us so often that they were sure it was the right thing to do that I got sick of hearing it; but Ben never wanted to listen. I think he just turned them off when they started talking about it. I told Elly about it and she said that was probably the only way Ben could handle it. Elly was pretty smart, especially for a kid who was a toy. After she said that, I felt pretty sorry for Ben. He was awfully little to have to understand such confusing things. Maybe he was afraid that every guy Mom went out with was going to be his next stepfather. Sometimes I'd get mad at him for being such a baby about it, but then other times, when I'd see how helpless he felt about the whole thing, my heart would melt for him. Then I'd start feeling resentful for having to feel that way about my little brother, when who was going to feel that way for me? So it was a pretty tough time for all of us.

All except Randy. Every day that he was at our house, he seemed to take over our family a little more. And with each new step, I grew more uncomfortable and Ben grew more furious. We should have known that it would have to lead to something terrible.

5

Did you ever notice the way things happen in bunches? You can go along for ages with absolutely nothing interesting in your life; then bim-bam-boom, everything in the world starts happening all at the same time. If it's good things, you can't even enjoy them as much as if they'd come separately; and if it's bad things, you can't handle them the way you could if you had more time. That's the way it was, starting just around the time we first met Margie. But the good things and the bad things were so mixed in together, sometimes I could hardly tell the difference.

The best thing that happened to me personally

was that I got to be assistant editor of the school paper. Now that I was in eighth grade, I felt a million years older than I had the year before. I started seeing a lot of myself in the kids I used to envy for knowing their way around and having so much self-assurance. Instead of their seeming different and like people I had to look up to, I felt like their equal now.

Elly was made story editor, and we got pretty friendly with the rest of the staff. The nicest part of that was Greg Forbes, the editor. He was a ninth grader, and for my money the most fabulous guy at Midland Junior High. Greg had the kind of looks I went for: pale and poetic, with a face carved out of ivory. But what I liked even better was his guts. He would stand up to anyone for whatever he believed in. I adored working with him and just about melted every time he praised something I wrote or how hard I worked on the paper. What he didn't realize was that I did it all because of him, and the more attention he paid to me, the more I did. But it didn't get me anything more than appreciation, because he was going out with Wendy Wolf. Elly and I had a theory that the neatest guys always chose the girls you'd least expect, and vice versa. It sure was true for Greg, because Wendy was very flashy-looking, with one of those phony smiles, too much makeup, and definitely weak in the brains department. I couldn't imagine what Greg saw in her, but Elly insisted, "That's what guys like Greg go for. It makes them feel smarter."

"That's stupid," I argued. "How can someone feel smarter with a dummy?"

Elly shrugged. "Since when are men logical?"

"Besides," I went on, "what about women? Look at my mom and Randy. I mean, there's another unlikely couple for you!"

"Yes, but it's the same thing I was saying," Elly insisted, "except the other way around. Women do it too, I guess. This is what your mom needs now."

I laughed. "Someone she's smarter than to make her feel smarter?" Elly laughed, too.

But none of those theories stopped me, because I knew I had nothing to lose by being Greg's secret groupie. In spite of Elly's theory, I was certain he was too smart not to wake up one day and realize what a fool he'd been not to pick me. And I intended to be around when that happened.

I thought it was happening the day he asked me if I would work with him on the series of editorials he was writing about renovating the gym. "We ought to do it at one of our houses," he said, "because we might not be finished at closing time."

"Oh, sure. Want to come to my house?" I clamped my mouth shut so he couldn't see my teeth chattering.

"Okay. How about tomorrow?"

I paused a moment, quickly checking out my busy schedule: let's see, I have done the whole downstairs and my room. "Sure," I said. The chattering had stopped, and I even managed to squeeze out a smile, as if it was every day in the week my dream guy asked to come over.

"Great! Suppose I meet you on the front steps after school—" I had to clutch the wall for support. "Oh, wait," he added, and his beautiful smile lit that always-serious face, "I'd better make it four o'clock at your house. I, uh, have something to do right after school."

Well, you can't have everything. Greg walked Wendy home every single day. He wasn't going to change that for me, not now. Not yet.

I let go of the wall, feeling steady again. "Four o'clock is better for me, too."

At least that way I'd have a chance to clean up Ben's after-school mess and work on myself before he got there. That night I baked a double batch of brownies and hid half; I didn't have enough time to read the history assignment, but I did all my other homework.

I didn't know how I was going to make it through the next day. Elly was excited with me. She didn't think Greg was all that great, but she liked him. "Except for his taste in women," she said, laughing her squeaky laugh. "Wow, what he ever sees in Wendy! Of course," and she winked, "now maybe he's getting older and wiser."

Ben and David were on their third round of brownies by the time I got home. "Hey, guess what, Jess," Ben cried as I walked in, "I'm co-captain of the soccer team!" His eyes danced with happiness.

"Oh, hey, that's great, Ben!" I hugged him, but he shrugged me off, embarrassed.

David grinned. "He's the first fifth-grader to make co-captain. Maybe next year we'll both be co-captains."

"I hope so." I was looking at the clock and wishing they'd leave before Greg came. As soon as they did, I flew around tidying up, then washed my face, brushed my hair, and changed my clothes three times, ending up with the same outfit I'd started with. By four o'clock I was waiting for the doorbell to ring, but the phone rang instead.

"Jess, was it today or tomorrow I was supposed to come over?" Greg's voice came faintly through the loud music in the background.

"Today," I said weakly.

"Oh. I'm really sorry, Jess, but I got mixed up. Look, would tomorrow be okay?"

"Oh, sure. No problem."

"Terrific. Let's see, about four, okay? This time for sure."

I threw the phone against the wall, and it made a terrible sound. Then I grabbed two brownies from the platter I had so carefully arranged on the kitchen table and shoved them into my mouth, practically choking as I battled the sobs working their way up. And in that moment the kitchen door flew open, and in walked Mom and Randy.

"See," Randy said, eyeing the platter of brownies, "I told you there would be some left for us!" He smiled at me. "Your mom said you and Ben would probably finish them off before we got here." He helped himself to one. "But I had faith in you, Jess. Mmm, these *are* good."

Mom went to the refrigerator for the milk, and Randy bolted down two glasses, then looked at me. "Want some, Jess?"

I shook my head. "Enjoy yourselves," I said and started to leave.

"Hey, wait a minute, I need you!" he called after me, and I turned around in the doorway. "Tell your mother here she shouldn't do it. She shouldn't be a cheerleader."

"A *cheerleader?*" I screeched.

He grinned at her smugly. "See, I told you. *No* one approves. It's a crazy idea, Ann, and it goes against everything we stand for."

My mind was made up very fast. "What do you mean? I think it's really neat! Is it true, Mom?"

"Well, yes, I wanted to ask you what you thought, Jess. They asked me today, and I thought why not, it sounds like fun, and it's something I always wanted to do in high school, so why not? You know how I love football. But Randy thinks it's dumb."

"What's dumb about doing something you've always wanted to do?" I asked, all innocence.

"Well, for one thing," Randy growled, stuffing another brownie into his face, "it goes against the whole spirit of what we agreed higher education is supposed to be about. That is," and he gave Mom a knowing look, "before she got taken in by that macho establishment crowd!"

"Now wait a minute," Mom began, but Randy went on, "And for another, she won't have enough time and energy left for the underground newspaper she was going to work on with me."

"Underground newspaper—what's that?" I asked.

"Remember I was telling you about it last week?" Mom said. "The one our group wants to put out to expose all the lies the administration is using to brainwash the student body about raising the tuition? We couldn't believe the garbage they've been putting in the student newspaper; and when we started asking the staff members about it, they said they got their facts firsthand. Randy tried to get them to see they were being duped, but they're just a bunch of dopey kids who go along with the system."

Randy was smiling proudly at Mom. "So our group decided to put out our own newspaper, with the real facts. But we need commitment from our staff, not people going off and doing something like being a *cheerleader*, of all things!" He shook his head in disgust. "How corny can you get?"

Mom turned and faced Randy with that determined look she gets when she tells Ben he can't watch any more TV. "Look, Randy, I don't care what you think about it. Jess is right. It's something I've always wanted to do, certainly more than working on an underground newspaper. Why, I don't even want to work on a newspaper at all! And I want to be a cheerleader, so I will. Besides," and now she turned to me, "we've already got one newspaperwoman in the family, and I think that's enough. You're really *good* at it, too." She turned back to Randy. "I have a great idea—why don't you get Jess to work on the paper with you?"

Randy's mouth dropped open; he looked pretty funny standing there with brownie crumbs stuck in his scraggly red beard and that surprised look on his face.

Ben burst in the door. "I have to find—oh, Mom, hi!" His smile faded when he saw Randy, then he glanced at the dwindling brownie platter. "Hey, you better not eat all of those. They're for *us kids!* Right, Jess?"

"Ben!" Mom cried. "How can you be so rude?"

"Oh, that's okay, Mom," he replied, "they're for you, too. Listen, do you know where my football helmet is?"

"I think it's in your closet," I said. "Ben, guess what? Mom's going to be a cheerleader."

He stopped in his tracks. "Honest?" Then he burst out laughing.

Randy smirked now. "See, didn't I tell you? Even Ben thinks it's a stupid idea. Right, Ben?"

My little brother stopped laughing and studied Randy's face for a quick moment, then said, "Stupid? I think it's fantastic! Mom would make a great cheerleader. Boy, can she holler loud! Don't you think she'd make a good cheerleader, Randy?" He ran off to his room and Mom and I looked at each other and burst out laughing.

"Ben is just rebelling," Mom told me that night when she came in to talk. "I don't know why he has this thing about Randy. Randy is so crazy about both of you."

"Oh, Mom, come on, he is not. Don't you see he's just trying to make you think that so he can hang around here and freeload?"

"Jess, I'm shocked to hear you say such a thing! Why, Randy is the kindest, most genuine, most honest person I've ever met. Sometimes I just don't understand you." She sighed. "Oh, well, I know it's not easy for you kids to have to share me. Of course, I know you understand, but Ben is still too young. That's why I want to do all these things for myself, Jess—so I'll be someone everyone can identify in my own right. Even that underground newspaper. Oh, I support the idea and everything, but I'm just not ready for that kind of commitment yet. Besides," and she giggled, "you're the writer of the family. I certainly don't want to be competing with you!"

That sort of gave me the creeps. Who ever heard of a mother afraid of competing with her daughter? Usually it's the other way around. Besides, I'd have switched into Mom's shoes any day in the week. I'd have given up everything to be as pretty, have a guy —even a nerd like Randy—follow me around like a grateful puppy, the chance to be a cheerleader, people begging me to work on something, even an underground newspaper. Who ever heard of someone like that afraid to compete with a nothing who broke out every month and whose biggest talent was being Miss Nice Guy.

That's what Greg called me when he came over the next day. Yes, he came. He got there at 4:01 and spent five minutes apologizing for the day before and then asked if I had anything to munch on; he'd skipped lunch to work on material for the editorials. I felt like flogging myself about the brownies that I had helped finish off and decided that was my punishment for not sticking to my faith in this wonderful, hungry guy. I managed to scrounge up some slightly stale blueberry muffins and made some hot chocolate. And then I blurted out, before I could stop myself, "You missed the brownies. I made a double batch the other night, but they went pretty fast."

He smiled that lovely smile. "Well, that's what I get for being so careless. I promise never to forget again if you promise to make another batch for the next time." He grinned. "Even a single batch will be okay."

How could I concentrate on anything serious after that? All I could think of was the remark about "next time." I kept studying that chiseled, classic profile as I sat next to him, thinking, "I've done it, I've finally done it!" He might have even broken up with Wendy by now. I'd be able to tell in school the next day. It was easy enough, because they always walked together, either holding hands or with his arm around her shoulder.

54

"Do you think we ought to stress the overemphasis on sports or the cut in our cultural programs?" His voice sliced through my reverie.

"Oh—how about both?" I said mindlessly.

He raised an eyebrow. "Both? How could we do—hey, wait a minute, that's a great idea!" He squeezed my arm in his enthusiasm, and I almost fell off the chair. Luckily, he didn't notice; he was too busy scribbling away. After that he just kept writing as fast as he could, stopping now and then to read me what he had written and waiting for my reaction, and then back to more scribbling. It was amazing the way his enthusiasm grew as he kept working. My brain was practically paralyzed. I was trying so hard to come up with zippy ideas. All I managed were two or three and the rest were his, but he kept saying, "That's great, Jess, you give such good feedback— I'd never be able to do this without you." I don't remember the other things he said, but those statements were engraved on my heart in golden script.

I got up a half-hour early the next day to work on my hair and even tried out some of Mom's mascara, but I needn't have bothered. I saw Greg after third period, when I usually saw him, and the way I usually saw him: with his arm around Wendy. I turned away fast, but not fast enough. "Hi there, Jessica," he called. "Great work session we had yesterday."

"Yes, wasn't it," I mumbled, wanting to disappear into the wall.

"Hey, what's this all about?" Wendy said, still

all smiles. It was perfectly obvious that she knew exactly what it was all about, which ruined it for me even more. If he ever did come again, I thought then, he'd probably bring her along.

"You sure give up easily," Elly said as we sat in my kitchen after school. "Now that you've gotten to first base, you're not going to throw in the towel and strike out, are you?"

While I was arguing about her mixed metaphor, Mom walked in. Elly and I both stopped talking and stared. Finally I said, "What in the world are you wearing?"

She looked innocently down at her pea coat and then farther down and burst into a smile. "Oh, yes, I almost forgot I still had it on."

"It" was the four inches of pleated skirt that was sticking out of her pea coat, then several more inches of thigh, and knee, then purple knee socks and saddle shoes. She flung open the coat to reveal a gold turtleneck sweater and gold skirt with purple pleats. The sweater had a big purple A in front, and Mom twirled around pertly to show off her costume. The purple pleats flared around as Mom flung her arms about the way cheerleaders do, and I just sort of groaned. Elly jumped up and threw her arms around Mom's waist, turning to me as she crowed in her creaky voice, "Your mother, the cheerleader!"

Yes, my mother, the cheerleader. And, the next day, my father, the bridegroom.

"I wanted you to be the first to know."

Daddy was pacing up and down the thick shag rug in his apartment. Margie was due in a little while, and they were going to take me and Ben to a sreet fair on the West Side. Ben jumped up and ran into the bathroom.

"I was afraid of that." Daddy looked upset. "I was hoping he wouldn't take it hard. . . ."

What about me? I thought, for the thousandth time that year. I couldn't even decide if I was taking it hard or soft or medium, but didn't anybody *care?*

"What about you?" I heard Daddy saying. He put his arm around me. "You like Margie, don't you?"

"Yes, sure I like Margie. So does Ben. It's not that, Daddy. I mean, I guess I'm glad for you, and Ben probably will be, too, when he gets used to the idea. It's just that—well, kids are never prepared to find out that their parents are going to get married."

"Yeah," Ben piped up from behind us. "How are kids supposed to feel when one day they find out their mother is a cheerleader and the next day that their father is going to get married?"

Daddy jumped up. "What do you mean your mother is a cheerleader?"

"Oh, didn't you know?" Ben said.

"Well, what's wrong with that?" I asked.

Daddy burst out laughing. "Nothing, I guess. It's just that I was surprised."

"Well, then," I replied smugly, "you can imagine how Ben and I felt with *your* news."

"Hey, I didn't tell you the best thing of all!" Ben cried. "I'm co-captain of the soccer team!"

Daddy's face lit up. "No kidding! Hey, that *is* great news! What about you, princess? Has anything special happened to you this week?"

Has it ever! I wanted to say. The guy I like thinks I'm smart and a good worker but not the girl he wants to put his arm around. But I just said, "Well, I told you I'm assistant editor of the school paper. Nothing big happened since that."

"Well, that's sure big enough to last," he said and hugged me. Margie came right after that, and we ended up having a really nice day together. Later we found out that Daddy had told Mom about him and Margie the night before, but asked her not to say anything because he wanted to tell us himself.

"Wow," Ben said that night, "Mom is getting pretty good. I never thought she could keep a secret so long!"

It was after we got home. Mom was out with Randy, and I had gone into Ben's room to say good night. I just laughed. But he was looking serious. "Hey, Jess, did you ever get the feeling that Mom was just another kid in the family?"

That's when I was really sure I was a mother: because I wanted to say, "Yeah, often." But all I said was, "Oh, Ben, stop being stupid and go to sleep!"

6

As I was saying before, about things coming in bunches: it was right after that that everything started happening, first sort of slowly, and then so fast I can hardly sort out even now which came when. I think if I get to be a hundred I won't ever be able to look back at those next couple of months and feel comfortable about them. Maybe in my old age it will give me something to laugh about, but now, when I'm fourteen, I still don't see very much that was funny. Except about what happened after Daddy's wedding.

First you have to know that Greg did come back to my house to work on those editorials, and I did make another double batch of brownies. This time with pecans instead of walnuts because once at a staff meeting he had mentioned how much he loves pecans. And this time the whole scene was set even better than before because I was more relaxed and self-confident. Well, not really relaxed, but more self-confident. I was ready to jump out of my skin with excitement. At four o'clock on the nose the door-bell rang. I waited a few seconds to answer it so he wouldn't think I was just sitting there waiting, the way I was. When I opened the door there he stood, all smiles; and there she stood, all smiles, too.

"Hi, Jess. I hope you don't mind that I brought Wendy along. She didn't have anything to do, and I thought she might be able to give us some good ideas."

I never knew till that moment how hard it was to fake a smile, and it was then I really appreciated Wendy's talent, because she seemed to do it all the time. Except after she tasted my brownies. "Oh, wow, these are fantastic!" she cried. She even rolled her eyes. "Greg, don't let me have another single one. But they're worth getting fat for."

"Ha, fat!" Greg snorted. "You? Maybe around your right knuckle." He ruffled her hair. "Enjoy yourself, pussycat." He turned to me. "Right, Jess?" He reached for the platter and took two more brownies, handing one to Wendy. Then he opened his notebook. "Okay, let's get started. Look, Jess, here's how I think we ought to pull them all together. I did a rough draft during study hall. Want to read it?"

They talked together very low while I read—each sentence over twice I was so distracted by the looks they were exchanging. It was a marvelous session. Greg started writing down our ideas, which were his echoed by my approval and Wendy's praise, and in an hour we had the whole thing done.

"That was just super, Jess," Greg said as they were leaving. "I sure appreciate your working with me on this stuff. You have a really good understanding of the issues."

"Thanks for the brownies," Wendy added. "See you in school tomorrow."

I shut the door fast so I wouldn't have to see how close together they walked, his arm around her shoulder. Then I rushed upstairs to my room, pulled my diary out of my desk drawer, unlocked it, and wrote: "I hereby promise myself that from this day forward I will hate, loathe, and despise Greg Forbes. I will never have him at my house again and I will only ever speak to him on business. Also, I will never bake any more pecan brownies in my entire life."

It wasn't hard to keep that promise because whenever I saw Greg we only talked about the paper. The only thing that rescued my social life was seeing that half the other girls at school didn't have a boyfriend either. But at Hallowe'en things started easing up because Lauren Kane had a costume party in her garage. There were as many boys there as girls, and Elly and I had a lot of fun, dancing practically all the time. After that we started hanging out with another bunch of nice kids, and one day I realized that I liked junior high very much. I had begun easing off on the housework way back in the spring, and now I was fighting with Ben all the time to get him to do his share. I even found myself telling Mom she had to help more. Between the two of them—Ben with his soccer practice and Mom with her cheerleading practice, and of course all her homework besides—they seemed to spend more time making explanations and excuses than doing any work.

And then, of course, there was Daddy's wedding. Daddy and Margie had planned a small Saturday afternoon wedding, but she was going to wear her mother's lace wedding gown. Nana thought it was awful because Daddy had been married once before, but Mom just laughed off the whole thing. I thought it was pretty neat myself. After all, Margie had never had a wedding and she'd always wanted to wear her mother's gown, so why shouldn't she? I happen to be a feminist myself, and I think women's liberation is women doing what they *want* to do.

It was when it got close to Thanksgiving that everything started going crazy in our family. Mom had become really involved in being a cheerleader and had done a bunch of games by then. She was pretty good, too. Elly and I went to a few, and we could see the improvement each time. In the first one she was like a stick, stiff and tight, but so were some of the others. You could tell which ones had done it in high school. Of course, there was something else, Elly pointed out: the age factor. After all,

Mom was just as cute as all the other girls, but let's face it, we both agreed, she *was* the senior citizen of the group. Elly and I decided they wanted to make a showcase of Mom to prove they didn't discriminate against age and race and all that. So considering everything, Mom held her own; and after Elly and I coached her for a few sessions, she limbered up a lot and made amazing improvement.

Ben never went to Mom's games because he always had his soccer games the same day, so half the time I went to those to root for him. Daddy and Margie came out to them, too, and Elly usually went and some of our friends who had brothers on the team. In no time they got on a winning streak, and Ben was walking around on air. By the time he found out they were going to play in the championship game at the end of November, you could hardly talk to him. Mom's team was losing a lot, and when we teased her about it, she got mad and said if her whole family came to root for *her* team maybe they'd win, too. Of course we knew she was kidding—we thought—but I had the feeling she was really a little jealous. I was sure of it the day she brought up the Thanksgiving Day game.

"Of course I'm not going to make turkey this year," she said to Ben when he asked. "It's our big game. I couldn't possibly. Besides," she added, "who ever heard of a cheerleader making Thanksgiving dinner? We'll go to Nana and Gramps—they're going to have the whole family and expect us, too. Just like last year."

Ben gave me this funny look, and I knew what he was thinking, because I was, too: last year had been our first Thanksgiving without Daddy. He had gone on a holiday cruise, so we never even saw him the whole weekend. Everyone had made a big fuss over us—our aunts and uncles and cousins, and of course Nana and Gramps. But by now everyone was getting used to Daddy not being around any more, and I knew there wouldn't be much fuss. And that's when it struck me: not only was everyone else getting used to Daddy not being around any more, but even Ben and I were. If someone had told me the year before that I would even think such a thing, I would have thought they were stark raving mad. It was like when you cut yourself, and the pain is so bad at first you don't know how you're going to stand it. And then after a while it isn't as sharp anymore; or else it's the same, but you've gotten used to it, so it seems better. That's kind of the way it was getting to be with having Mom and Daddy split up.

"I think she's rebelling," Ben told me that night, after Mom said she wasn't going to cook. "Don't you think this whole cheerleading thing is going to her head?"

I laughed. "Mom would do anything to get out of making Thanksgiving dinner. Remember how she used to complain about it every year?"

Ben looked suddenly glum. "Daddy used to be in charge of the turkey, remember? All she ever did was the trimmings."

I smiled at him, pitying his ignorance. "But that was the biggest part, silly!" I knew what he meant, though. That probably *was* the reason Mom didn't want to do Thanksgiving—how dumb of me not to see it! On top of that, the Saturday after was Daddy's wedding, so I realized it was a tough time for her. I was glad at least she had her cheerleading to see her through. Of course, she had Randy, too, but he was sort of mad at her for leaving him stranded with his underground newspaper. Ben was so happy not to have him around much any more that he kept telling Mom she ought to stick to her work and sports and not bother with that stuff, it wasn't her style. Of course, everyone knew how Ben felt about Randy, so we just laughed when he said those things.

We had school only in the morning the day before Thanksgiving, and I got home just a minute before Ben walked in the door. He was white as a ghost.

"What's wrong?" I asked, rushing over to him. When he was little he always used to get sick the day before our vacation trips and we'd have to postpone them. Now I could only think of Daddy's wedding in three days.

"I made a terrible mistake," Ben said. "Our championship game. It's this Saturday."

"Oh, no!" I held my head. "Are you sure? How could it be? You knew it was Daddy and Margie's wedding!"

"I know, I know. I got mixed up with the dates.

I thought our game was the next Saturday."

"Oh, Ben, that's terrible! What are you going to do?"

"Well, I can't miss my own championship game, can I?"

"But Daddy's wedding! When will you ever have the chance to see your father get married again?"

"You never know," he said.

"Ha ha. Listen, what time is the game?"

"Two o'clock, same as always."

"And the wedding's at one, in Brooklyn. With a reception afterwards."

"The worst part is, Daddy and Margie'll have to miss my big game! Remember they said they wouldn't miss it for anything? Maybe they'll change the wedding date!" He ran to the phone. "He'll figure something out, I know he will!"

"Oh, Ben, you're crazy!" I called after him. "What can he do now? It's all arranged."

Daddy was in shock at first. He said he couldn't possibly change the wedding date but if we'd give him time, he'd think of something. "Just hang on. I'll call you Friday and let you know what we'll do," he told Ben.

"Are you sure he said that?" I asked. "If he can't change the wedding plans, what can he possibly do?"

Ben shrugged. "I don't know, but he said he'd think of something. And you know Daddy, he always keeps his promise."

I looked at Ben with all the pity in my heart. Growing up was painful, didn't I know. And this little kid was soon going to have the disappointment of his life.

But first, there was Thanksgiving. It was a raw day and we just didn't feel like going to Mom's game, so we went over to Nana and Gramps' house early and had fun with our cousins. The house smelled so good from all the cooking and baking and there was such a fun holiday spirit that when I went into the dining room to check on the napkins for Nana I was surprised to see Ben standing by himself looking out the window.

"Hi, what're you doing?" I said.

"Oh, nothing. Just thinking."

"Don't strain your brain."

"I wonder if Daddy's having a nice Thanksgiving," he said then, his voice odd.

"Of course, he is! He's with Margie and her family, and . . ." I trailed off, not knowing what else to say.

"Yeah, and not with us. Thanksgiving is for families. *Whole* families."

"Don't be a baby, Ben!" I muttered and ran out of the room. Because I knew he was right. But when I saw him next, he was in a hot game of Slam with our cousin Billy, and soon everyone was told to get ready for dinner. We were all starving by then, but Mom hadn't come yet. She had said she'd be there by four, and at a quarter past Gramps finally said, "Well, we might as well sit down at the table and get started on our soup. I'm sure Ann will be here any minute, and she won't mind."

Well, we had our soup, and still no Mom. Then Nana said we might as well go on with dinner, Mom could easily catch up; so out came all the goodies, and we all dug in. Halfway through, there was a funny bumping sound at the front door. Uncle Stan jumped up and hurried over to open it, and there stood this hulk of a man carrying Mom. He was wearing a football uniform, and her left arm was in a sling. In a flash everyone crowded around them, all talking at once.

"I broke my arm," Mom explained. "It was that darn flip in the new cheer. I lost my balance and fell, and Sandra tripped over me and my arm got broken. It's in a cast."

"Oh, darling, are you all right?" Nana cried, her voice shaky.

"Yes, Mother, I really am. They fixed me up in the emergency room and gave me something for the pain. All I am is hungry. Gee, I'm sorry I'm late, everyone."

"But honey," Gramps said now, "I don't understand. It's your *arm* that got broken, not your *leg*. Why is this man carrying you?"

She sort of burrowed into his shoulder. "I was just so shaky, and it was hurting so much. Oh, everyone, this is Augie Strohl. He's our middle linebacker, and he won us our game today." She introduced everyone, then said, "Do you have any dinner for us?"

They were quickly led to the table, where Aunt Betty set an extra place next to Mom's. Augie was still carrying Mom, and he sat her down ever so gently. He was seated next to Ben, who immediately tackled him with such a barrage of conversation about football and soccer that Gramps finally had to rescue him.

Augie drove us home, and Ben asked if he'd like to come in for coffee.

"That sounds great," Augie replied. "If it's no trouble."

"Oh, that's right," Ben said. "Mom's arm. That's okay, you can make it, Jess."

"Thanks," I said, and we all laughed. I had never seen Ben take to any of Mom's friends the way he did to Augie, and I couldn't help wondering if he liked him for himself or because he was competition for Randy. Mom and I giggled about it together later, after Ben was in bed.

"What's going on, Mom?" I said then.

She shrugged. "I don't know, Jess. Augie has been hanging around a lot lately; and when this dumb thing happened today, he was right there and took me down to the hospital and waited through the whole thing while they set my arm and everything. He was an absolute angel. I've never paid much attention to him before; but we spent so much time together today, I got to know him pretty well and I really respect him a lot. He's young, but he's very mature. His father died when he was twelve, and he's been helping out in the family ever since. He's so responsible and serious. And sensitive, too. You'd never think that of a college football player. See,

Jess, that's why I always tell you, you just can't make generalizations about people."

"Hey, wait a minute—*you* told *me* that?"

She laughed. "Oh, maybe it was you who told me. That's right, it was when we were talking about Elly, and I said it was a miracle she isn't a spoiled brat. Anyway, we both agreed that you just can't generalize, and we were right."

"Well, what are you going to do next?" I asked her.

"Next? About what?"

"About Randy."

"What's to do? Randy and I are still good friends, but that doesn't mean I can't see other men. Randy is free to see other women, too. We don't have any claims on each other."

"Will you go out with Augie if he asks you?"

She nodded. "Of course. Tomorrow night. He wants to see me Saturday, too, but I already have a date with Randy."

I shook my head. "Oh, Mom, you're really something. By the way, how's your arm?"

"It's starting to hurt again. I'd better take some aspirin. I'm beat, Jess, I'm going to bed. Sweetie, I'll need you more than ever now. You'll even have to help me dress and undress. Ha! Now you'll be *my* mother!"

"What else is new?" I said before I could stop myself.

"What did you say, Jess?"

"What happened to your sweater? How did they get it off you?"

She shuddered. "Oh, don't remind me—it was awful! Augie called his sister, and she brought this shirt over to the hospital. Well, anyway, I can count my blessings—at least it's not my right arm. I'll be able to do most things." She gave me a funny smile. "Except housework and dressing myself."

I laughed. "And cheerleading."

Her mouth opened soundlessly, then she frowned. "Why? Do you really think I'll have to give it up, Jess?"

Even with Mom's flair for the dramatic, she finally had to admit that she wasn't going to be able to make it as a cheerleader with her arm in a sling. The person who suffered most from that was Ben, because it sent her right back into Randy's waiting arms.

But that wasn't till after the wedding.

7

The phone woke me up the next day. "What do you mean, everyone's asleep!" Daddy gasped. "It's eleven o'clock!"

"Well, I'm awake now. We had a really big day yesterday."

"Oh, that's nice," he said absently. "Margie and I had a nice day, too. But I missed being with you and Ben."

"We missed you, too, Daddy. But I didn't say a nice day, I said a *big* day. That's why we were sleeping late. It was pretty nice," I added.

"Anything wrong?"

"No, except Mom broke her arm." I told him

what happened, then asked if he thought Ben would be able to come to the wedding.

"That's why I'm calling, Jess. I want you to go wake up Ben and put him on the phone. And you listen, too, so you're all sure to understand."

"Okay," Ben said sleepily into the phone, "what's the scoop?"

"Well, you're not going to believe this, but I worked out something that's going to have you at my wedding, and me and Margie at your soccer game without changing hardly any of the plans."

"Oh, great!" Ben cried. "You changed the date!"

"No, and not even the time."

"You're right, Daddy, I don't believe it," Ben said.

Daddy laughed, then went on, "Well, we'll be cutting it close, but I guarantee it will work. All you have to do, Ben, is wear your soccer uniform underneath your suit. Are you on the extension, Jess? Now listen closely, both of you, and don't forget a thing: like I said, Ben, wear your uniform under your suit, and bring along your knee pads, your socks, and your sneakers in a bag. And be sure to bring that bag in to the wedding with you, because we're going to the soccer game in a different vehicle from the one you're coming to the wedding in."

"Oh, yeah?" Ben said sleepily.

"Yeah," Daddy said. "Jess, do you have that straight? Ben sounds as if he's still asleep."

"Oh, yeah?" Ben said again. "I'm to wear my

73

uniform under my suit and bring my knee pads and sneakers and socks in a bag and be sure to bring them in to the wedding with me because—"

"Okay, okay," Daddy cut in, laughing. "You do better sometimes when you're sleepy than when you're wide awake."

"Hey, Daddy, what's this vehicle going to be, anyway?" Ben asked.

"Well, you just wait and see," Daddy said.

"But we'll never make it to the game in time if your wedding's at one o'clock and my game is at two." Ben sounded really wide-awake now.

"And what about the reception?" I asked.

"Oh, yes," Daddy replied. "That's the one thing I was able to change. It's going to be after your game."

"I still don't see—" Ben began.

But Daddy cut in, "Seeing is believing. Now you kids just be ready to be picked up at eleven-thirty tomorrow morning. And I give you my word, Ben: we will deliver you to your soccer game by not a minute later than two o'clock."

Ben and I tried to figure out all kinds of ways we could make the trip from Daddy's wedding at Margie's parents' house in Brooklyn Heights to Ben's soccer game, normally a forty-five minute drive.

"If the wedding takes fifteen minutes and there aren't any traffic tie-ups, we can do it!" Ben said.

"Oh, Ben, who ever heard of a wedding taking fifteen minutes?"

His big blue eyes held puzzled surprise. "How long do weddings take, anyway?"

74

I shrugged. "It depends, but certainly more than fifteen minutes."

"How many weddings have you been to?" he demanded now.

"None, but—hey, isn't this weird? The first wedding we're going to in our lives is our father's!"

"Yeah. But right now all I'm interested in is if it'll take more than fifteen minutes. After all, how long does it take to say "I do" twice and put a ring on a finger? Listen, *I* know! He's renting a helicopter!"

"Ben, don't be crazy. You know Daddy can't fly!"

"No, dummy, I mean renting one with a driver —a pilot—and all. You know, the way you do for fishing boats."

I laughed. "Well, I guess it's possible. What about a hydrofoil?"

"Hey, yeah, wouldn't that be neat! Do you really think so, Jess?"

We couldn't have been more wrong, but talking and wondering about it helped both of us not to have to think about the wedding itself, and the fact that Daddy was really getting married. That now we were going to have two mothers, when one was almost more than I could handle. And that probably someday we would have two fathers, too. That night while I helped Ben pack his bag for the next day, he put it into words:

"The thing of it is, Jess, I like Margie, and all, and she'll probably be okay to live with whenever we stay with them. But what about Mom? What'll it be like if *she* gets married? What if she marries some creep who likes to boss us around?" I just looked at him, trying to think of what to say. But before I did, he went on, "What if she marries Randy?"

"Oh, don't worry, Ben, she won't. He's just a passing phase in her life. After all, she's out with someone else at this very moment. I have a feeling Randy isn't going to last long."

"I sure hope you're right." He smiled then. "Yeah, it's true, Augie sure is crazy about her. Now someone like *him* wouldn't be bad. But Randy! Forget it! I wouldn't even stay around long enough to find out what it would be like."

"You're being silly, Ben," I said, but chills went through me. I'd never really thought about it in that way. Ben wasn't such a dumb kid. I mean, I didn't hate Randy the way Ben did, but I sure didn't want to *live* with him.

When Margie's brother Steve came for us the next morning, the first thing Ben asked him was how long it had taken him to get there. "I made terrific time," he replied, looking at his watch. "Fifty minutes on the nose. I hope we do as well on the way back."

"*Fifty minutes!*" Ben shrieked, turning to me. "It's got to be a helicopter!"

"No, no, this is a car," Steve said, smiling. He was only about nineteen and real cute.

"Listen," Ben said, "do you know about the plans my father made to get me back to my game on time?"

Steve hit the side of his head, groaning. "Oh, do I know! I think it's a hot-air balloon."

Ben looked at me in desperation, his lower lip trembling now. "See, it's all a joke! I'll never make it to the game on time!"

Steve patted Ben's knee as he maneuvered the car with his left hand. "Don't worry, kid, you'll make it with time to spare. Your dad swears he has it all worked out, but it's a big secret and no one knows how."

"Does your house have a big roof?" Ben asked him.

Steve shrugged. "I don't know. I mean, average, I guess, for that kind of house."

"Big enough for a helicopter to land on?"

Steve roared with laughter. "Nope, I'm afraid not."

"Do you live near the ocean?"

Steve was still laughing. "No, not really. But I'm sure it's not a boat. And I'm pretty sure it's not a helicopter. We'll just have to wait and see."

Margie's parents' house was a brownstone on a pretty street. Steve dropped us off right in front—there were big yellow cones there so no one could park—and Daddy came running out to bring us inside. He was all dressed up in a fancy black jacket and gray vest and gray-and-black-striped pants and one of those wide gray-and-black-striped ties. He looked very handsome.

Inside, the house was one of those old-fashioned places with a lot of polished wood, and it looked very elegant. There was a miniature organ in the corner of the living room, and all the furniture was pushed against the wall. The rest of the room was set up with rows of red velvet folding chairs. A huge garland of all different kinds of beautiful white flowers decorated the fireplace, and the dining room was set up with a bar and people were in there having drinks. Daddy's three brothers and their wives were there, and of course Margie's parents and sisters and brother and Daddy's and Margie's close friends and Ben and I. The judge who was going to marry them was Margie's parents' best friend.

At a few minutes before one o'clock, we all sat down on the folding chairs, and a man began playing the organ, and then all of a sudden there was the wedding march. Everyone turned around toward the stairway, and there at the top were Margie and her father. She looked beautiful in her mother's long white-lace gown. There was a little crown of flowers in her hair but no veil; she was hanging onto her father's arm for dear life as they slowly came down the winding, carpeted stairway. I wondered if she looked so scared because she was getting married, or if she was afraid of tripping. But when they got to the living room safely and Daddy stepped out to take her father's place, she smiled, and I felt kind of shaky inside as she took Daddy's arm.

There were two bad moments at that wedding. When the judge asked is there anyone here who thinks this marriage shouldn't take place, Ben put his bag down on the floor and started to get up. I was just about to grab him when I saw that he was only straightening out his seat. He must have leaned back or something and it had started folding up, so he had to get up to fix it. Then, when it came to the ring part, as Margie held out her left hand to Daddy, I thought it was lucky *she* hadn't broken *her* left arm. That's when I started giggling. People turned around to look at me, and I wanted to die of shame. Ben poked me, but then the organist started playing and I got a tissue out of my bag and pretended I was coughing into it.

Everyone crowded around Daddy and Margie, and then they made their way toward me and Ben. Daddy took hold of Ben, who was still clutching his bag, and Margie grabbed my hand, and we all rushed toward the door that Margie's father was holding open for us. Suddenly Margie stopped, turned, tossed her bouquet at her sisters, and then lifted her gown so she could really run. Just as the four of us got through the doorway, a big shower of rice came raining down on us, and we raced down the steps and across the sidewalk with rice falling out of our clothes and our hair. Daddy stopped us at the curb, and parked there was a red-and-white ambulance, its lights flashing. On its side in large gold letters was:

FIDELITY PRIVATE AMBULANCE SERVICE.

"Okay, folks, this is it!" Daddy yelled, pointing to the back doors, which were standing open. "Hurry, get in. The guy I rented it from guaranteed to get us to Flower Field by two o'clock."

Ben and I scrambled inside while Daddy lifted Margie in; he yanked the doors shut and bolted them like an expert. At that same moment, the ambulance was on its way, its lights still flashing and its siren shrieking.

"What time is it?" Margie gasped.

"One-thirty on the button. Ben, get yourself out of that suit and into your socks and shoes and knee pads. You've got to be ready to walk out of here and onto that field in playing condition."

I think Ben's mouth had been hanging open all the time, but no words ever came out till now: "Daddy, how come you didn't get a helicopter?"

"No place to land it close to the house."

"Oh, yeah," Ben said thoughtfully as he started unbuttoning his jacket, "that's what I figured." He looked at me. "Steve was right. The roof isn't big enough."

I don't think I'll ever forget the looks on the faces of Ben's teammates when our ambulance pulled up to the field and we started piling out: first Ben, complete in his soccer uniform, then Daddy, in his bridegroom suit, then Margie, in her white lace wedding gown, and me, bringing up the rear, clutching Ben's bag with his good clothes and shoes. Some grains of rice dripped from each of us after we straightened up, but I don't think anyone even noticed that. They were too busy staring.

Coach Sommers came rushing over, and he

grabbed Ben's arm. "We thought you skipped out on us! You're just in time. One minute to two."

Daddy was grinning at all of us. "See, didn't I promise you?"

Margie was beaming up at him. "Oh, Pete, you're marvelous!"

The driver had gotten out, too, and was closing the back doors. "Well, we did it, didn't we, Mr. Cromwell. I told you not to worry. If traffic had been lighter, we'd have been here two minutes sooner. Which team do you think will win?"

"Foolish question," Daddy replied, laughing. "We'd better hurry and get seats. Want to join us? You can park the ambulance over there."

"I'd love to," the driver said, "but I'm on call."

"I never knew you could rent an ambulance for something like this," I said as we hurried toward the bleachers.

"You can't," Daddy said. "Let's just say this was something very special."

"You might say," Margie put in, "a matter of life and death."

Ben's team won by two points, so you can see it was a pretty exciting game. And one that nobody there will probably ever forget, because besides all the kids' friends and families in their usual Saturday knockaround clothes there was this crazy family dressed up for a wedding—us. All the people we knew crowded around and made a big fuss over Margie and congratulated Daddy. I had this nagging feeling someone was missing and then remembered it was Ben, who was busy with the game. But soon I realized it was more than Ben. It was Mom. And then, of course, I understood how crazy *that* was. I thanked my lucky stars she hadn't decided to show up.

But no, Mom was busy that day keeping herself busy so she didn't have to think about what was going on. She had come into my room after her date with Augie the night before but I had been too sleepy to have much of a talk with her. All I remember was that she'd had a really nice time and she liked Augie a lot but thought maybe he was a little young for her. It wasn't till I was thinking about it later that I remembered he was only a few years younger than Randy. I decided it would be a point I could push.

"It's not the years, Jess," Mom explained the next day after Ben had gone out. We had told her all about the wedding-and-game spectacular and she had laughed herself silly over the ambulance and Margie coming to the game in her wedding gown; but she had had a funny look on her face about the rest of it. I shifted the subject to Augie and Randy, and when she said again about Augie being sweet but too young, I pointed out the few years difference between him and Randy.

"I know Randy is young in years, but he has lived so much, knows so much of the world. He did all his growing up when he was a little boy."

"So did Augie," I said. "Remember he was saying how he took over after his father died?"

"Yes, but that's different. It's a matter of personal and social maturity, Jess. Randy has traveled so much, he's done so many things. And now he's making a big splash at college with his underground newspaper! Poor thing, he's taken on more responsibility than one person ever should."

"Well, no one made him do it," I said, afraid of what was coming.

"No, of course not. Just the way no one makes you breathe. Jess, there are some things in life that just need to be done. And there are still committed people, thank heavens, who are unselfish enough to do them, no matter what the personal sacrifice. But there's only so much one person can do."

"So you're going to be one more person to help him out."

Her smile was broad and bright. "That's right, Jess. After all, I have to have something to take the place of cheerleading. Oh, you were right about that, sweetie—I can't possibly go on with it with this darn cast. So I decided I might as well use my energies where they can do some good." She looked a little sheepish as she added, "I'm glad I was a cheerleader because now I know what it's like. But I've gotten it out of my system—Randy made me see that last night—and now I'm ready to devote myself to the important things in life."

"Like Randy's underground newspaper."

"Oh, that's only a small part of it, Jess. That's just a medium for expression to try to shake the establishment out of the stranglehold it has over all the people who trust it."

"Mom, what's got into you? You sound like one of those crazies who go around ranting and raving about politics."

"Now wait a minute, Jess. I know I get carried away, but it's such a basic need we want to serve: Insuring the rights of all citizens to get what's coming to them and not being brainwashed by the big-money interests. We have to participate in shaping our destiny!"

"Well, yes, but—what are you going to do?" I asked, totally confused. "What are you going to *be?*"

She looked at me in a dreamy haze. "Jess, I'm going to be an activist."

"An *activist?* Mom, what are you talking about? An activist about *what?*"

"Why, about everything that needs to be acted on! It's about time this family started getting involved in social issues instead of all that middle-class stuff like soccer games and cheerleading and parties. There's a whole world of disadvantaged, exploited people out there, and the time has come to take some responsibility for helping to change things."

"But I still don't understand, Mom. Exactly what is it you're going to *do?*"

"Well, I'm not sure yet," she said a little weakly. "I have to talk to Randy about it some more." She laughed. "I started out planning to break off with him last night, but I ended up letting him talk me into going back with him."

"What about Augie and the other guys you were starting to see?"

"Well, I didn't make a total commitment. Randy wanted me to, but I'm not ready for that yet. That's when he started in on me about becoming an activist. He's coming over later, and we're going to discuss it more. All I know is he made me see the light, and I know for sure I'll never be passive again. I always just let things happen to me. From now on I'm going to help them happen."

"That sounds pretty good," I said, "if they're the right things."

She hugged me. "Leave it to you to get to the heart of things. Well, I promise, Jess, I'll devote myself to a cause that will touch our lives very closely. I'm moving out from behind the scenes into the forefront. Just watch me, Jess!"

I watched. We all watched. Ben and I and Nana and Gramps and our friends. We couldn't help watching, because Mom was transformed all over again. She started having meetings at the house and would be up half the night catching up with her studies because she'd spent so much time organizing watchdog committees and doing research for the underground newspaper and helping Randy with all the other work that went along with getting it written and printed and distributed. They would take one problem at a time and really hammer away at it: the college admission policies; where the college got its funds; that kind of thing. Half the time I didn't even understand what they were driving at, and I hated to ask because the answers were long, boring lectures. The bad thing about it was that Randy was around the house more than ever; the good thing was that lots of other people were, too. Mom even got Augie involved, but I think he just did it because he wanted to be with Mom. I was glad, anyway, because it's the only thing that kept Ben from exploding about Randy.

Actually, we didn't see much of Mom alone, those days. And it was sure a good thing I had gotten used to doing most of the housework and taking care of Ben. Because she didn't have time for any of that. She was busy being an activist, keeping up her grades, and finding a place for herself that made her feel good and important. We can laugh now, but while it was happening our nice, crazy little life suddenly turned into a nightmare.

8

It was right after the lull of all the holidays and winter vacation. During that time I spent practically all my spare time at Elly's house and tried not to pay too much attention to Mom and her nutty friends. That's what Ben and I called them to each other, but never to Mom. After all, we could see that in a lot of ways they were good for her. They were a pretty mixed group, some really nice and attractive and some grunges, some pretty immature and some just the opposite.

Mom's arm healed nicely, and she made a big party when the cast came off. There were some regular-age students there, some "dropbacks" like Mom, and even some professors. Mom told me and Ben that we could each bring a friend, but we said no, we'd rather not. Instead we spent that weekend with Daddy and Margie.

They were settled into their new garden apartment in Queens with an extra bedroom. Ben and I liked staying over with them. Margie was still working, but she loved to cook and bake and fuss around the house. Once Ben asked me, "Doesn't Margie remind you of the way Mom used to be?" He was right. She always got all dressed up to go out with Daddy. And she'd started collecting recipes and cutting out those household hints from the newspaper. She had even learned how to change the washers in the faucets. "I never did a thing when I was growing up in my parents' house, and after I got my own apartment, I missed all the things my mom and dad did for me. But I really never had the time to learn to do them till now. I didn't know it was so much fun!"

I remembered the way Mom had complained about doing all those household chores; she didn't think they were fun. But she had never had an interesting job in an advertising agency like Margie, so housework and children had been her job, and a lot of the time it wasn't fun. It was nice to see Daddy so happy, too; but every time we'd come home from their place, Ben would say things like, "It's not that I don't like Margie, but I'd still rather have Mom and Daddy back together." And I'd say things like,

"Well you're just going to have to get used to it this way."

"Another thing," Ben said, just before everything went berserk at our house, "at least Daddy stays the same. But Mom! She's like a different person every month. I liked her when she was a cheerleader much better than since she got to be an activist. Boy, if only she hadn't fallen and broken her arm. We would have seen the last of Randy for sure. Jess, let's think of something to get rid of that guy."

The next day a nightmare began at our house. It was the day of Mom's sit-in.

Mom and Randy and their group had been at war with the college ever since it had announced plans to cut back on financial aid and to raise the tuition. Mom's group had organized a really strong campaign to fight it and gotten lots of students involved. They had formed committees to meet with the college officials, and they had written all about it in their underground newspaper, which was becoming a big popular thing at the college. Mom and Randy were getting to be practically celebrities. But the officials wouldn't change their plans, so the students had decided to have a giant protest rally and demand a change. Mom told me to make the leftover chicken for myself and Ben for supper that night and not to wait for her because she was sure to be home late. Not that that was anything new.

"In fact," she said, "it might be very late, so don't worry. I'll call when I can to let you know what's happening. And please make sure Ben gets to bed on time. Oh, and Jess, if Nana or Gramps call, don't say anything about the protest rally. I don't want them to worry. Just tell them I had to work late on a project at school."

So I did what she said. I put the leftover chicken in the oven and sprinkled bread crumbs and grated cheese over canned stewed tomatoes and put that in too, and heated canned corn. For dessert Ben made chocolate sauce for our frozen bananas. He was getting to be pretty good around the kitchen, but I always had to argue with him to help clean up. We were just finishing KP when the phone rang. I ran for it, saying, "That's Mom, she said she'd call." But it was Gramps asking for Mom, and I followed her instructions.

"What kind of project?" Gramps asked, and before I could think of an answer he went on, "I just heard on the radio that there's all kinds of trouble over at the college. A protest rally—it must be your mother and her crazy friends. Did she say anything about it to you?"

"Well, not exactly—"

"Now, Jessica, I want the truth. Did she tell you not to say anything to me?"

"She didn't want you to worry," I said weakly, too worried myself to hide anything from Gramps.

"Well, I'm going right over there and see what's what. It sounds like a bunch of maniacs have taken over the administration building, and I want to make sure my daughter isn't one of them."

I begged Gramps to take me and Ben along, and Nana came too, but we couldn't get near the administration building. The police had it cordoned off, and there were people milling around all over: students, professors, and just people. The students were yelling and carrying all kinds of signs with slogans and demands. In a way it was almost like a street fair. Every now and then we heard loud chanting coming from the building, and then a bunch of policemen would run toward it and up the steps. Policemen blocked all the entrances. Meanwhile the students kept circling around the building and then coming back to meet in groups.

I was getting pretty nervous, and Gramps went over to a policeman and started insisting to be let in to get his daughter; but before the policeman could even answer Gramps, a bunch of students closed around us, and I knew right away what they were going to do. Without a second thought I knew what I was going to do, too. I joined their circle as they rushed past the policemen, through the barricades, through the police on the steps, and into the building. It was one of the biggest moments of my life.

We raced down the hall toward the nearest room, and it was like being swept along by a wave. Everyone in my group was yelling, and the noise coming at us from the room was like a roar. Inside there were so many people I didn't know where to start looking for Mom. They were sitting around on the floor and on desks and counters and windowsills, and some were laughing together while others were yelling out the windows: "One two three four! We are ready for a war! Five six seven eight! We won't pay a higher rate!"

I started pushing my way through to search for Mom, and all of a sudden a big cry went up. I spun around to see a bunch of policemen burst into the room. Now their yelling rose over the students' voices, but I couldn't make out what they were saying. Someone was standing on a desk right next to me screaming, "Who let them in?" and I looked up. "Randy!" I yelled, tugging at his pants leg, and in the same moment I heard Mom's voice screaming, "Jess!" She was standing in front of me, her face flushed with excitement, her eyes sparkling. "Sweetie, how in the *world* did you—"

"Sit down!" Randy yelled through his cupped hands now, and everyone else started passing it along as they all dropped to the floor, sitting cross-legged with their arms folded. More police were pouring in, and they started dragging the students out. "Don't move!" Randy was screaming, and most of them listened to him and just sat there. "Remember, C.D."

The police started picking them up off the floor and carrying them out, and Randy yelled, "Ann, Jess, get down!" Mom pulled me down to the floor, and we sat there like the others. Just as Randy started crouching down on the desk, three cops came over and surrounded him. One swung his nightstick right near Randy's face, and Randy sprang up and punched him.

"Oh, no!" Mom screamed as a whole slew of cops rushed over; then I never even saw what happened to Randy because I was so busy with Mom. She had started to get up but fell over in a funny way. I grabbed her arm. "Mom, this is dangerous, let's get out of here!" There were flashbulbs popping all over the place—it felt like the whole town was in that room by then. But Mom didn't budge, or even talk. That's when I realized she had fainted.

"Okay, young lady, if that's the way you want it," a policeman snorted next to me, picking up Mom's still form and carting her off, the way the other cops were picking up the seated, motionless students. By the time I scrambled up, an ocean of blue-uniformed men had come between us. I pushed and shoved my way through the crowd yelling, "Wait, wait, you can't take her away, she fainted!" And one of the cops turned to me and said, "Cool off, kid, that's just what they do when they practice civil disobedience." He and his partner bent down and picked up a girl just the way they had picked up Mom, and the girl went limp and they carried her off. I was shaking and crying by now and had reached the door, and as I ran down the steps, there was a whole caravan of police vans lined up and they were shoving the students into them. Flashbulbs were still going off a mile a minute, and police officials were calling out orders through bullhorns, and I flew down the steps without even feeling them under my feet. By the time I got to the lined-up vans, half of them were closed and pulling away, and just as I felt about to faint myself, Gramps appeared.

"Jess!" He grabbed my arm and pulled me over to the side. "Did you find your mother?" Now Ben was standing there, and Nana.

"We saw them taking Randy into a van!" Ben was squealing. "He looked a mess. Where's Mom?"

"They took her, too!" I sobbed. "She fainted when Randy punched the cop, and they thought she was just going limp, and . . ." I burst out crying, and Nana looked as if someone had bopped her over the head. Gramps started pulling at all of us, pointing us toward the car. "Come on, hurry up! They'll never get away with this!"

Gramps went through all the red lights when there were no cars coming. There weren't any cops left to stop him, they were all at the college. It looked as if all the cops in the state were at the college.

The police station was like a crazy house, but Gramps just shoved his way through without even waiting for the rest of us. Boy, he sure was in good condition for a grandfather! By the time we caught up with him, he was talking to the sergeant at the desk. The sergeant was smiling at him, and when we got there we heard him saying, "Oh, yeah, that's the one that fainted in the van." He signaled to another officer and said, "How's the little lady who fainted?"

Some of the men and women who were hanging

around the desk crowded in to listen, and as I cried, "She didn't faint in the van!" I noticed a couple of them writing in notebooks. "She fainted in the office up there, at the college," I went on, my voice shaking. "And the policeman picked her up and carried her out. They wouldn't even *listen*—"

The sergeant turned to me. "How do *you* know?"

"Because I was there. She's my mother. I went in to get her, and when she fainted—"

"Your *mother?*" the other policeman repeated, looking me over. The men and women who were there listening moved in closer, and now I noticed the microphone one man was holding up. A woman who had been taking notes asked me, "Why was your mother there?"

"She was part of the protest," I said.

She exchanged a funny smile with the man holding the microphone. "Oh, really?" she went on. "What, uh, *group* is your mother with?"

I heard someone say something about "outside agitators moving in," but I didn't know what they were talking about and I didn't care. All I wanted was to get Mom out of this mess. I said, "She's with the students, of course. She's a sophomore."

"At the *college?*" the microphone man asked.

Suddenly Ben was there, and he piped up, "Yeah, didn't you ever hear of mothers going to college? This isn't the Dark Ages, you know!"

Everyone cracked up at that; but the policeman

I was talking to went over and crouched in front of Ben, the way grownups do to little kids when they want to be the same size. "Oh, so that's your mom, too?" he asked him; and when Ben nodded, he said, "Is your name Ben?" When Ben nodded again, he said, "Hey, you have a funny mom, all right. When she came to in the van, do you know what she said? She said 'Is this an ambulance?' " Ben and I exchanged a knowing smile. The policeman went on: "And do you know what she said next? She said, 'Are you taking me to Ben's soccer game?' "

Mom made out much better than Randy in every way. Gramps got Mom out right then and there; and I think they were glad to see all of us go because Gramps got all excited and threatened to sue for false arrest. Mom was very upset because they booked Randy and sent him to jail for socking the policeman, and he had to stay there till someone came up with bail for him. Mom was going to try to make some arrangements the next day. Gramps told her she was crazy, and they had a big fight about it all the way home in the car; but when we got to our house she grabbed him, threw her arms around him, and sobbed, "Thanks for coming to my rescue, Dad."

He was all smiles. "Well, it was really Jess who came to your rescue."

"Oh yeah?" I said. "I did her as much good as a rabbit in a lettuce patch."

They all laughed. "But you found her and led us to her in captivity!" Gramps said.

"Did you see all those reporters and TV people around?" Nana asked. "It'll be all over the papers."

"And TV!" Ben cried, rushing to turn on the set.

The whole thing was on the local ten o'clock news. There were scenes outside the administration building and then from inside. And sure enough, there was Randy punching the policeman and—

"Look!" Ben screeched. "There you are, Mom! Yeah, you really were fainting, weren't you!" Then they showed how the police picked up the students from their sitting positions and another flash scene showed them loading into the vans, and *then:*

"Lookee, Gramps, there you are!" Ben was howling and Nana gasped as Gramps shook his finger in the sergeant's face. Now there were Ben and I and the man with the microphone, and my very own fourteen-year-old celebrity voice came over the TV in our living room loud and clear: "She's my mother. She's with the students, of course. She's a sophomore." Then the camera swung to Ben, who was saying, "Yeah, didn't you ever hear of mothers going to college? This isn't the Dark Ages, you know!" And then there was a shot of Mom as she rushed toward us. She looked like one of those ads in a magazine of a college student modeling jeans and a yellow turtleneck sweater.

"Well," Nana said when it was all over, "you can see who the orphan is in *this* family. I'm the only one who didn't get into the act!"

"Just wait till tomorrow." Gramps groaned. "You'll be in the act, all right. Everyone in the world is going to be at us about this." He turned to Mom. "It was bad enough that you had to go off to college, but now this! Ann, it's too much. You've got to find yourself some new friends."

"Dad, I may be a college student, but I'm a grown woman. I don't need your approval of my friends."

Nana put her hand to her head and wailed, "I can't believe this. Everyone here is acting like a teenager except the only one who *is* a teenager!" She turned to me. "What about you, Jessica? Why don't you put *your* teenage two cents in?"

I shrugged. "What's there to say? It's up to Mom to do what she wants."

"That's right!" Mom said. "I don't need *anyone's* approval—not yours and not even Jess's and Ben's."

"Well, it's a lucky thing," Ben snorted, "because you sure don't have mine!"

That turned out to be the understatement of the century. The story and pictures were all over the newspaper the next morning, and right smack in the middle was the now-famous shot of Randy punching out the law and Mom fainting. I was a big celebrity in school and could hardly get through the halls, everyone was stopping me so much to talk about it. By the end of the day I was so tired of answering questions I couldn't wait to get home. Ben was a celebrity too, but in a different way. All the kids at his school thought it was the funniest thing they ever heard, having a mother who almost got arrested at a sit-in and whose boyfriend punched a cop. He was embarrassed to death and said he wasn't going to school the next day. Luckily, it was a Friday. We knew that by Monday he'd cool off. Luckily, too, we were spending the weekend with Daddy and Margie.

They took us bowling and to a movie and a karate exhibition and a Greek restaurant with belly dancing. Ben brought the newspaper along, and the first night he told Daddy about everything that had happened. Daddy didn't say much, but he looked upset. And then when Ben started going on about Randy and how he hated him and he didn't think Mom ought to have anything to do with someone like that, Daddy gave him a little lecture about how Mom was free to do whatever she wanted, and it wasn't up to Ben or me to decide who her friends should be. "After all," he pointed out, "you kids have had plenty of friends that we weren't crazy about, but we didn't tell you to stop being friends with them just because we didn't like them. If they had been harmful to you, it would have been a different story—"

"But Randy *is* harmful to her!" Ben said. "Look at all that dumb stuff that went on, and it was all his idea." He looked at Daddy accusingly then. "Nothing like this ever happened when you lived with us. Why can't it be like that again?"

I wanted to smack Ben, but I left the room instead. By the end of the weekend he wasn't talking about it anymore, and by the time he left for school Monday morning it seemed as if he'd forgotten about it. I hoped he had.

9

Mom and some of her friends went crazy trying to raise the bail money for Randy. There was a whole to-do among the activist group that staged the demonstration because they had decided to use non-violence, and Randy had violated the agreement when he punched the cop. A big block of students left the group because of it, and Mom found herself in charge of the whole bail business. But she came through, working her special magic; and after two days of frantic activity, she sprang Randy from jail late on Saturday.

He wasn't at the house the whole next week; and I was glad, because Ben seemed pretty calmed down about the whole thing by then. Mom was all excited because the demonstration had accomplished a lot: the student group was having meetings with the college officials to try to work out a solution. Mom came home late every day, and I kept her dinner warm for her, the way she used to for Daddy when he'd get home late from the office.

On the Monday of that same week, a cold, bleak day, Ben and I watched the after-school movie on TV. The story was about a teenage girl in Maryland who was so upset when she found out her parents were getting a divorce that she ran away from home. She took a train to New York and met some young people, who let her stay with them, and then the story got all complicated about her getting in trouble. Meanwhile, her parents were frantic and started this gigantic search campaign. It had a double happy ending: the parents not only found the kid and brought her back home, but they got back together because of what they went through and canceled the divorce plans. Actually, it was a pretty interesting story, and right in the middle Ben was so involved he tipped his chair all the way back against the wall and I caught him just as it was collapsing. "You dummy!" I screamed. "You could fracture your spine that way! Don't you know by now?"

"Shhh!" he hissed. "I know, I know; but I *didn't*, did I?" He sat down again, more carefully. "Let's not miss the rest of this, okay?" I was surprised that Ben was so interested, because he usually didn't have the patience to sit through that kind of drama. I didn't think much about it, though, even when he asked me afterwards if a person could get divorced more than once. And even when the next night he came into my room while I was doing my math and handed me his electric pencil sharpener, which he had gotten for his last birthday, saying: "Here, you might as well have this. I never need it, and you're always coming into my room to use it."

At breakfast on Friday, Mom told us there was a concert at the college that evening, and she was going with Randy. "So don't wait for me for supper," she said.

"Oh, I was going to tell you," Ben said, "David and I have a Cub Scout meeting after school, and he wants me to go home with him after and have supper there. I was supposed to ask you and tell him in school today." Ben and David often exchanged visits like that, the way Elly and I did.

Mom looked at me. "Do you mind staying alone, Jess?"

"Oh, that's okay," I said. "I'll ask Elly to stay and we can fix something together for supper. We were going to work on our math together after school anyway."

""David said his father would bring me home at eight o'clock," Ben added.

"That sounds good," Mom said. "But be sure you don't get back any later."

After Elly left that night, I went into Ben's room

for a ruler and I couldn't help but notice how neat it was. He had straightened it up without anyone's yelling at him about it. Like Mom, I decided, he must be going through a new phase. But then I noticed that it was past eight-thirty and remembered Ben was supposed to be home at eight, so I phoned David's house.

"What do you mean?" David's mother said when I asked if Ben had left yet. "He hasn't even been here."

I quickly found out that Ben had never been to David's house at all. That he had never been expected. That there wasn't even a Cub Scout meeting that day. That Ben, in fact, had not been in school that day, so David had assumed he was sick. "I'll be right over," Mrs. Burns said. I felt sick.

I phoned Nana and Gramps, certain Ben had to be there, but of course he wasn't. They said they were coming right over, too.

"But shouldn't we call the police?" I asked.

"I'm going to call them right now," Gramps told me. "And while you're waiting for us, I want you to look up the phone numbers of every one of Ben's friends."

Before I did that, I called Daddy. At first he thought I was joking, but he pretty soon decided that I wasn't. "I'll come right over," he said, his voice shaking. "Have you called the police? Where is your mother?" I answered his questions and then said it might be a better idea if he stayed home in case Ben tried to get in touch with him.

"Maybe he was kidnapped," Daddy said. "Yes, Jess, maybe you're right. I'll stay here by the phone."

"Kidnapped!" I screeched. "Who would want to kidnap Ben? We're not rich! Besides, I think he ran away, Daddy. The other night he gave me his electric pencil sharpener, said he never uses it anyway. And *then*, he cleaned up his room, without anyone telling him to."

"Jess, I just got an idea. Go into his room right now and see if there's any money in his bank. I'll hold on."

I hadn't thought of that. Ben had a bank that was made like a little safe with a combination lock, and it was heavy with quarters he had been saving for a year. I didn't know the combination, but I ran into his room and climbed up to get the bank from its hiding place on the closet shelf. It was there, all right. But I didn't have to know the combination to open it. I could feel it was empty. Then I looked in his dresser drawer where he kept his most precious possession, a Boy Scout knife. Gone. So was his toothbrush. I hurried back to the phone to report to Daddy, and then the doorbell rang.

The doorbell seemed to keep ringing the whole night, and the telephone, too. Mr. and Mrs. Burns arrived first, and right after them the police and Nana and Gramps. I started making out the list of Ben's friends' phone numbers, and Nana got some pictures of Ben for the police. The neighbors began coming in then because they saw the police car. Two detectives arrived; and after they got the report from the policemen, they left, and the detectives started asking me all about Ben.

Daddy called back and spoke to the detectives, and afterwards they started asking me a million questions, about all the things I had told Daddy and a lot of other stuff about what Ben did and said and how he acted all week. One was standing, but the other was sitting on that little chair near the TV, and when he started tilting it back, I cried, *"That's* it—it was that TV program!" I remembered how Ben had tilted the chair back too far when he was so involved in the story, and I started describing the program about the girl who ran away from home. Everyone was listening now, and I didn't want to go into all that stuff about the divorce, but I suddenly remembered what Ben had been saying to Daddy about why things couldn't be the way they used to be. And then I remembered Ben asking me if a person could get divorced twice. It clicked: Ben ran away because he figured it would bring Mom and Daddy back together, the way it did in that story! Then Daddy could just get a divorce from Margie and come back to Mom, and things would be the way they used to be.

The detectives told us they were going back to headquarters to send out a Missing Person alarm and contact the Runaway Squad in New York, and they asked me for Daddy's phone number. As soon as they left, I went upstairs to call Daddy and told him my theory.

"It makes sense," Daddy said. "Listen, I'm going downtown to the bus station and the train station to look around. I can't stand just sticking around here waiting. Margie will be here to answer the phone, and I'll keep checking back with her and you."

For the next couple of hours our house was like a beehive. People were coming and going, the phone was ringing, but there was no word of Ben. Nana sat in the corner just nodding when people spoke to her but not answering at all, and Gramps kept pacing the floor and running to the phone to call someone whenever he got another idea of where to look for Ben.

I went to my room and cried a lot, but every time the front door opened, I'd run downstairs to see if it was Mom. I kept trying to think of the best way to break it to her, but when she finally got home, at eleven-thirty, I was up in my room crying and I heard this thumping on the steps and suddenly Mom was beside me on my bed with a wild look in her eyes. "Tell me it's not true, Jess!" She was sobbing, shaking me. "Tell me it's just a joke."

I burst out crying, and then she broke down, and we sat there bawling and hugging each other.

"If you two don't get hold of yourselves," came a familiar voice from the doorway, "you're just going to make everything worse." I looked up to see Randy, leaning casually against the door jamb, smiling that know-it-all smile of his.

"How can we make it any worse than it is?" I asked.

He shrugged. "If you're a basket case, you won't be able to help out when you're needed."

"He's right, Jess," Mom said, wiping her eyes. "It was such a terrible shock to come home and find everyone in the world in my house and then get this news. Oh, Jess, what could have happened to him?"

"He ran away," I said numbly, telling her then the story about the TV program and my theory.

"That's about the dumbest thing I ever heard," Randy said. "Just because he saw that program! He's probably pulling some stupid trick just to get you going."

Mom, looking as shocked as I felt, said, "What are you talking about, Randy? You can't be serious!"

"Never was more serious in my life. That little bum," and he chortled now, "he really knows how to get at you! I always noticed that about him—never seems to be able to get enough attention."

Mom's gasp cut the air like a knife. "Randy, how could you say such a thing? He's only a *child!*"

"Yeah," he snorted, "some child! With a pretty fiendish mind, I'd say, to pull something like this."

"*Pull* something! Oh, Randy!" Her voice changed from shock to cold fury. "Do you realize something terrible might have happened to Ben? Did that ever enter your infantile brain?"

"Hey, now wait a minute, Ann, I know you're upset, but—"

"You bet I'm upset! And you're just making everything worse. You seem to have a talent for that.

I think you'd better leave, Randy. Right now, before I say something I'll be sorry for."

"You already have, Ann. Look, I'm really sorry for your trouble, but you're right. I think we'd better cool it for a while. The vibes have been getting pretty bad lately; I noticed that." He left, and Mom raised two clenched fists to her cheeks.

I turned and buried my head in my pillow, but I didn't cry any more. I didn't have any tears left. Besides, I had thought of something so funny that I promised myself it would be the first thing I'd tell Ben when I saw him again: "You did it, Ben, you did it! You finally drove Randy away!" Yes, when I'd see him again. *If* I'd see him again. . . .

The next thing I knew the phone was ringing. I jumped up, but it had stopped. That's when I realized I had dozed off for what had seemed a little while but was really hours, because it was ten after four. Mom was yelling something, and then I heard Nana and Gramps's excited voices. I shook my head to be sure I was awake and raced downstairs. Mom was just hanging up the phone.

"They've found him!" she screamed to me. Nana and Gramps already knew, and they were holding each other, laughing and crying. I whooped a yell and grabbed Mom, and we danced around, hugging each other.

"Where?" I gasped. "When? Who?"

"Asleep in the back of some restaurant in Penn Station. Just a little while ago. The New York police.

I'm not really sure about any more except that he's okay, and Daddy's bringing him home."

"Who was it who called?" I asked.

"Your father," she replied. "He said they found him, but he was right there, something like that. I didn't understand, but he said he'd explain everything when he gets here. The police are driving them to his place so he can pick up his car and come out here."

"You'd better get on the pipes and call our police out here," Gramps said.

"And the Burnses, too," Nana added.

"So late?" Mom asked. But after she called the police station, she phoned everyone else—David's house and the neighbors who had come over. We saw the lights going on in the houses all over the block and knew everyone was as happy for us as we were. Oh, I couldn't wait to get my hands on that baby brother of mine so I could kill him. Wait—just *wait* till I told him the good news!

10

"What in the world are you *doing?*" Nana asked Mom, who was pulling pots out of the cabinets and all kinds of stuff out of the refrigerator.

"I'm going to make lasagna," Mom answered, filling a big kettle with water. "It's Ben's favorite. I'm sure he's starving, and—oh, my gosh, I wonder if he's had anything to eat all day!"

"But it's almost five o'clock in the morning!" Nana cried. "Whoever heard of anyone starting to make lasagna at five o'clock in the morning?"

"Whoever heard of anyone *eating* lasagna at five o'clock in the morning!" Gramps chimed in, and I cracked up. But nothing stopped Mom. She started barking orders at me to help her get the lasagna made, and I was just as glad to do it. Even Nana and Gramps joined in. We were all hyper, and the last thing we could do was sit around and twiddle our thumbs till Ben got home. By the time we heard them at the door, the kitchen was steamy with good smells of sauce and garlic bread, and the table was all set, even with wine glasses.

Mom got to the door first, just as Ben walked in, followed by Daddy and Margie. Ben looked so strange, so little and helpless. I clenched my fists at my sides, as if that would keep the lump in my throat from exploding into sobs. Daddy came over and put his arms around me and held me close, saying softly, "It's all okay, Jess baby, it's all okay." He knew! I had thought no one could tell how I felt, but now I saw that Daddy really knew.

Mom rushed at Ben, but he stepped back and said in a croaky voice, "Hi, everyone." The four of us made a circle around him, while Daddy and Margie stood back, and we all began jabbering at once. He just stood there blinking and opening his mouth as if to talk, but nothing came out. Finally Nana got hold of him, patting his hair back and then giving him a peck on the cheek as she said, "Goodness, darling, we're so happy to see you, we're all at you at once, not letting you catch your breath. Why don't you just come over here and sit down—"

"Oh, that's okay," Ben said weakly. "Sorry I gave you guys a hard time. . . ."

Mom jumped into the small silence. "Never mind, honey, we're not going to talk about that now. We're glad enough that you're safe and back with us."

Ben was sniffing the air. "What's that smell?"

"I knew you'd be hungry!" Mom cried. "I made all your favorite things!" She grabbed his hand and pulled him toward the kitchen. "Look," she said when they got to the stove, "lasagna! And garlic bread!" She whipped open the oven door and a cloud of garlicky fumes rushed out. Ben jumped back, wrenched away his hand, and whirled around, facing all the rest of us as we stood watching in the doorway. His face was an awful greenish-gray, and he bolted past us, but he didn't make it. He threw up right in the hallway.

Nana went upstairs with him and got him washed up and into bed. Mom was looking pale and tired now, and Margie said, "Why don't you go and rest, Ann? You too, Jess. You both look exhausted."

"I am," Mom replied, "but I'm still too wound up. And you'll never believe it, but I'm starving."

"Me too,' 'Daddy said, "but not for lasagna and garlic bread."

"Well, I must admit it doesn't appeal to me right now either," Mom said, laughing. "It's almost breakfast time, anyway. What about a big round of scrambled eggs?"

Everyone liked the idea, and soon the kitchen was bustling with workers again. Daddy made orange

113

juice, Margie and Gramps fixed the eggs, Mom put up the coffee, and I toasted the English muffins and set out the marmalade. It was like one big, happy family, this bunch of kitchen elves, and I had to laugh to myself at the idea, considering what a strange kind of happy family it was: one father, one mother, and one stepmother, plus the grandparents and a couple of kids. Everyone was very friendly with everyone else —it was almost as if we were in the habit of visiting like this and fixing meals together. Of course, the only thing they talked about was Ben and what had happened.

Daddy waited for Nana to come down till he told us his story.

"After I talked to Jess, I took the subway to Penn Station and looked all over for Ben, every place I could think of. Whenever I saw a policeman, I whipped out his picture and asked if he'd seen him; and half of them already knew about it because it had gone out on the teletype and they were keeping an eye out for him. Then I went over to the bus terminal and did the same thing. No luck, back to Penn Station, in and out, up and down the streets, asking store owners and street people if they'd seen him. I never knew how big New York was till last night. I kept phoning Margie to find out if there was any news, then I went back to look again, for I don't know how long. Finally I went into a snack shop in the station for some coffee to keep me awake. Now this is the part you're not going to believe, because I still don't. I was drinking my coffee and trying to decide if I should have a doughnut with it, and the guy was standing there patiently—you know, the counterman—waiting for me to make up my mind, when we heard some commotion from the back of the shop. He said to excuse him a minute and went in back where the ruckus was, and then I heard him yelling, something like, 'No, how would I know? I wasn't back here since I came on.' Then something like, 'It's the morning man does the baking.' I heard some other muffled voices—it was real quiet, I was the only customer in the place. There weren't many people in the whole station, four in the morning. Now I hear a kid's voice, chirpy-like, then these other men's voices, and they're all getting louder as they come from the back into the shop, now I see these two big guys laughing and saying, 'Maybe we ought to give him some coffee to wake him up good and proper,' and then I hear this voice tweeting out, 'No, I *hate* coffee,' and then I hear this same voice: 'Hi, Daddy. They didn't tell me you were here.' "

"You mean it was Ben?" I squealed.

"No one else—your wacky brother. The two men were detectives from the Runaway Squad; they found Ben asleep on top of some flour sacks right inside the back door of the coffee shop. The same shop where I was sitting out in front having a cup of mud."

We all started bombarding Daddy with questions: how long had Ben been there, what had he done all day, how did he feel about being found, did he run into any trouble, how did he act afterwards; and Daddy told us as much as he knew.

"He looked mighty bedraggled, and he was pretty discombobulated because he had been fast asleep. He told me he had been hanging around the Penn Station area ever since the time his train came in, people-watching and reading his comic book and having a feast on all the junk food you can buy around there. He had twenty dollars on him, that little rascal, after he bought his train ticket, so he figured to stick it out as long as his money held out. Meanwhile, he was fortifying himself with strawberry twizzlers and potato chips and soft ice cream. No wonder he turned green when he smelled your gourmet meal." He grinned at Mom, who laughed but looked as if she was going to cry.

"What a story!" Gramps said. "Well, no one's happier than I am to see the little scamp back safe and sound—but I wouldn't let him get off so easy he thinks he can just pick up again whenever it suits him."

Daddy wasn't smiling now. "Well, I suppose you're right, in a way. But I don't think we need to take it out of his hide, because by tonight he was pretty miserable. Guaranteed he would have been on the first train home in the morning if those detectives hadn't found him. He found out pretty fast it's not so easy—and sure not much fun—to be a ten-year-old kid alone in New York."

"But why did he do it?" Nana asked, her face clouding over. "Why did that poor baby run away from home?"

116

"When I asked him," Daddy replied, "he just said he *had* to." He dropped his eyes. "I think Jess's theory was right. That TV program about the kid who ran away because she didn't want her parents to get divorced must have triggered it." He looked up and around at everyone. "Did Jess tell you about it? About how afterwards he asked her if a person can get divorced more than once? This way he figured I would—would do that, and come back to his home again."

Mom wiped her eye, Nana sobbed, Gramps looked away, and Margie laid her hand over Daddy's.

"Well," I burst out, "if he's going to be stupid, I don't know why everyone's letting it get to them. I mean, he's only a little kid, and he's just going to have to learn the way things *are*."

There was a long silence, and then Margie cleared her throat and said, almost in a whisper, "We have some news that might solve Ben's problem."

My head started to buzz, and I didn't know if it was from being overtired or from the excitement of what I knew must be Margie's news: she and Daddy *were* going to get divorced, and he *was* going to come back and live with us again! I looked at Daddy, who was watching Margie with a funny expression, and then I looked at Mom, who seemed unable to absorb any more dramas. Suddenly I remembered that time before the divorce, when both of them were so unhappy and everything was so cruddy at our house—the way they would talk to each other through us kids, and the fights they'd have and how Mom cried all the time and Daddy was always angry. After it was over, they started making new lives for themselves and then they got to be so different, especially Mom. I had always dreamed of the day when they'd see the light and get back together and we would be a happy family again, but now I saw that that was just a fairy tale and it wouldn't work. Daddy and Margie seemed so happy together, and Mom was so happy being a college student and building a new future for herself. Was it all going to go down the drain because of that dumb TV program?

"We're going to have a baby," Margie was saying.

I closed my eyes and leaned back in my chair, catching myself just before it tipped over—a family weakness.

"Wonderful!" "Congratulations!" echoed all around me; and as I looked at everyone and saw the genuine pleasure on their faces, I breathed a sigh of relief.

"Now he will know," Daddy said, smiling at me, "that that's the way things *are*."

"It's not all that easy," Mom was saying. "I've been giving this a lot of thought all night, and I realized if Ben is so troubled that he ran away from home, then he's got to get some help to get over this."

"Help?" Gramps said. "What do you mean? You heard what Peter said—he's home now and not likely to cut loose again so fast. . . ."

"I'm talking about professional help," Mom said,

her face set with that grim determination that wouldn't let her be talked out of an idea.

"Professional help?" Daddy repeated. "You mean like psychiatry?"

"Some kind of therapy," Mom said. "Little kids like that don't just pick up and take off for New York if they don't have some deep-seated emotional problem."

Gramps shook his head. "I knew she shouldn't take so many psychology courses."

"No, maybe Ann is right," Daddy said. "I'll go along with whatever you think is best, Ann."

Mom calmly folded her hands on the table. "I've been thinking it over carefully. I believe the three of us could benefit from counseling, Ben and Jess and I. After all, if Ben has a problem, then we have a problem, too. Family therapy is much more helpful to a child in situations like this."

"You're probably right," Daddy said, then turned to me. "What do you think, Jess?"

I was in total shock. *Therapy.* Where did Mom ever come up with such an idea! I didn't like it at all, not for *me*. "I think it's dumb," I said, then put my head down on the table and started to cry.

Daddy patted my head. "That's all right, honey. You don't have to do anything you don't want to."

I guess it was my nerves. And being tired, and mixed up, and scared. It's not easy being fourteen to begin with, when all your friends seem to get suddenly grown up and you don't; when people treat

119

you like an adult one minute and a toddler the next. The worst part, I guess is, your family. At least *my* family. It seemed that ever since Mom and Daddy split up, Ben was always the baby and I was always the grownup, and Mom was something different each day, somethng always in-between. At first it was fun for me, being so important in her life, helping her make decisions. But now I was getting too confused. Daddy was married to someone else, and they were going to have a baby; Mom surely would get married to someone else one day, and she'd probably have a career, too, and then she wouldn't need me any more. Ben would be the only one. I sighed. After I put Mom through college, she'd just have to be on her own, because Ben was going to need me. If he ran away from home at ten, what would become of him as a *teenager?*

We slept till almost four o'clock in the afternoon, Mom and Ben and I. It was weird going to bed just as it was getting light out and waking up in broad daylight, only for it to start getting dark an hour later. By the time I finished my shower, Ben and Mom were sitting at the kitchen table drinking orange juice, and there were cheese sandwiches sizzling on the griddle.

"Well, good morning!" Mom said brightly. "Or afternoon."

"Or evening," Ben added, laughing. "Hey, you look nice even with your hair all wet."

I smiled at him. "You look nice even with yours

all dry." Now I rushed over at him, grabbed him halfway off his chair, and hugged him so hard he yelled.

"Hey, kids," Mom cried, "don't get carried away!" But she was grinning and, like Ben, I knew she was loving every moment of it. Because even with his yelling, Ben was hanging onto me and not letting go. We had both saved it up for a long time—since he stepped in the door the night before. Finally, Mom came over and pulled us both to her, murmuring, "My two babies, I don't know what I'd do without you!"

"Babies!" Ben yelled, jumping back with a horrified look, and Mom burst out laughing.

"It was just a figure of speech," she said, hurrying over to turn the sandwiches. "Jess, I was telling Ben about the concert I went to last night, of futuristic music. Wow, it seems like two years ago."

I laughed. "It should seem like two years *from* now. What in the world is futuristic music?"

Mom got that serious look she puts on when she starts exploring deep subjects. "Well, you see it's . . . it's . . ." She burst out laughing. "I don't really know. It all sounded pretty weird. . . ."

"Yeah," Ben put in, "one of the guys opened the piano while the other one was playing and dropped little Styrofoam balls inside."

"Honest?" I said.

Ben shrugged. "That's what she told me. Were you making it up, Mom?"

"Of course not! Ask Randy if you don't believe

me. Oh, no, you can't ask him. Anyway, how could I ever think up such a thing myself?"

Ben shook his head. "Beats me. Hey, why can't I ask him?"

"Oh, he won't be coming around here any more," Mom replied, slipping the sandwiches onto the plates. "We broke up."

Ben bolted out of his chair like a shot. "You *what?*"

"You mean you didn't hear the big news?" I said. "It was the first thing I was going to tell you when you put your foot in the door—I can't believe I forgot about it!"

"Neither can I!" Ben cried. Mom was being very busy getting the milk out of the refrigerator and finding napkins and not looking at either of us; but we hardly noticed, we were so excited exchanging the news. "When did that happen?" Ben asked. "Is it for real?"

I shrugged, trying to give him a warning look, as I said, "Last night." After all, he and I might have been thrilled, but after all, it *had* been Mom's boyfriend, and people are always heartbroken when they break up like that. Ben ignored my warning look, even if he caught it, and started whooping and yelling with joy, crying out, "That's the best news I heard since I got back!" Mom just looked grim now, and when Ben finally calmed down she said, "There's even better news than that for you, honey. You're going to be someone's big brother at last." Her smile was so fake I cringed.

Ben stared at her. "What are you talking about! Are you going to have a baby?"

Now Mom's laugh was real. "Oh, no, that's all I'd need! No, Ben, Margie is."

"Margie is . . ." he repeated dumbly, ". . . is going to have a *baby?*"

Mom's laugh froze on her face, and I tensed, too. It was tell-it-like-it-is time, the moment of truth when Ben would have to know that his fantasy of Mom and Daddy getting back together and us all living happily ever after couldn't happen now—or ever. I was shocked that Mom threw it at him like that, that she didn't even try to break it gently.

"Hey, that's *fantastic!*" Ben cried. "Now I don't have to be the baby of the family any more!" He shook his head in amazement. "Well, what do you know? Someone else's big brother!" He glanced down at his plate, picked up the grilled cheese sandwich, and biting off a piece absently, said, "Mmm, this is good. First square meal I've had in a long time. Hey, I got to tell you about this man who has his office in a phone booth in Penn Station."

Mom and I looked at each other and burst out laughing.

"What's so funny about that?" Ben asked.

The period of tension had passed, and we were both relieved at how Ben had taken the news. I wondered how he would take the next little gem, about going for therapy, and when she was going to tell him about *that.* Knowing her, it would probably be in the next minute. But it wasn't.

"Were you really terribly upset with the idea of therapy, Jess," she asked later when Ben was up in his room, "or was it because you were tired and strained from all that happened?" She fixed me with one of her searching looks that forced out the truth.

"I guess both. After all, Mom, just because Ben has a problem, I don't see why *I* have to go for therapy! I mean, I can understand your wanting to go along, being his mother and all, but I don't know why you have to drag me into everything."

She came and put her arm around me. "Like Daddy said, Jess, you don't have to do anything you don't want to. At least, anything like that. But . . ." And then she went on to explain, in a new patient, teachery way, that if one member of a family has a problem it's everyone's problem; and if everyone goes for help together, it's much easier to solve the problems. And that way we'd each be made stronger for each other, and all that baloney. I kept looking at Mom while she was talking, and suddenly started seeing how much she had changed—all these new ideas that she'd gotten on her own, and now she was going ahead and making decisions without even asking me beforehand! I wondered if it was that psychology course she was taking this semester that she was so crazy about.

"Besides," she was saying, "you're going to be going through a period of big changes yourself, Jess darling, and as mature and wise as you are about other people's problems, I'm sure you're going to be stumbling on some of your own that you won't have such an easy time with. This kind of counseling will help you in so many ways, give you a lot of strength."

It was almost as if she had read my thoughts earlier that day after my big emotional scene, read all the lines of my doubts and fears about myself. But still, Mom was only a sophomore, and she needed me to see her through this tough period of her own life.

"Oh, all right," I told her. "I still think it's a dumb idea, but I'll do it for your sake."

11

Mom immediately started looking for the best place that we could afford for our therapy. She went about it the way she did her research papers, putting practically everything else aside till she found what she wanted. Anybody else would have been amazed at the amount of time and energy she used, but it's just what I expected from seeing the way she'd been operating ever since she started college: when she's onto something she considers really important, everything else goes by the boards, including eating and sleeping, till it gets done. Of course, this usually starts just before whatever her deadline is, so that's why she has to go nonstop like that.

Me, I'm different: I start on a project right away so I won't be stuck at the last minute, and all along I'm worried sick I won't make it on time. But I always finish early, sometimes so early that when I go over it, I decide it's no good and start doing it over, and then the squeeze is *really* on. So I suppose in a way Mom's method is better, because she only does it once. Besides, it's the kind of thing she's best at. She always excelled at making arrangements for things that can be done right then and there. She's probably so good at it because she loves doing it so much.

I can just see her someday with a big, executive job, sitting behind a huge desk, droves of people filing in with their problems, and her picking up one of the five telephones that are clustered on her desk and starting to call the White House and the British Embassy and getting things all straightened out. I can see her, too, being a social worker, going around seeing people about their awful problems; and after talking with Mom for a while and her telling them what to do and how to solve things, I can just see how they suddenly start to smile and feel better. Then she makes a few arrangements to get them started, and their lives just pick up immediately. That's why I think it's so important for Mom to get through college and get going with her life, because once she has it all together for herself, she's going to be dynamite.

Anyway, she started things rolling right away, and in a few days had an appointment set up for the following Wednesday. The thing that really surprised me was the way she told Ben about it, something she *wasn't* good at. I thought she'd just blurt it out, and I cringed at what might happen then. But she was incredible. She broke it to him so gently that he didn't really know what it was all about. I don't know if he *still* does. He never really had the chance to find out.

"We're going to talk to someone about ourselves and our family tomorrow, Ben," she told him at supper on Tuesday.

"What for?" He sounded bored.

She shrugged. "Oh, just about our feelings, our problems—"

He suddenly looked interested. "Who's *we?*"

"You, me, Jess."

"What about Daddy? Is it about him and Margie?" He paused. "The baby?" His face got pink.

Mom smiled. "Not really. I mean not especially. It's just about all of us as a family. What might be bothering us about each other or our lives."

"Boy, that sounds really stupid," he said. "Do I have to go?"

"Yes."

Suddenly he looked wary. "Hey, it's not about —I mean, it doesn't have anything to do with *Randy*, does it?'

"Randy?" she repeated, looking a little tense. "Why, no, why should it?"

"Are you sure?" When she nodded, he went on:

"Well, okay then—then I'll go." Mom relaxed and he smiled, getting up as he added, "But I hope it won't take long. I have some important things to do. Anyway," he threw over his shoulder as he left the room, "I think the whole thing is *really dumb*."

"What do you think he meant about Randy?" she asked me.

"I don't know—I guess maybe he was afraid you were going to break some news about you and Randy."

"Oh-h-h," she let out slowly, "I see." Then she shrugged. "Well, that's just one more complication out of my life." She smiled a little sheepishly, and I smiled back with relief.

"Mom, what did you ever see in him?"

"Oh, Jess, every relationship is worthwhile, leaves you a better—or smarter—person." She laughed. "I guess sometimes you're just better because you *are* smarter. Anyway, Randy and I did a lot for each other, but it was time to move on."

That smile was fishy. "Mom, are you involved with someone else?" I didn't add "already," the way I was tempted to.

"Well, I don't know if you'd exactly call it *involved*. . . ."

"Who is it, Mom?"

She blushed, but her eyes were sparkling. "Dr. Reynolds. Dante. My psychology professor."

"Oh, so *that's* how—*that's* why . . ." I should have known there was a reason Mom had wrapped up this project with such superefficiency!

"I can't wait for you to meet him, Jess. He's so wise, so compassionate. So *stable*."

"How old is he?"

"Exactly six months older than I, to the day. Our signs are perfect for each other!"

Well, I thought, *here she goes*. I braced myself for everything that I knew would come with it: the talkathon at bedtime, the ups and downs of the good and bad days, and the "What do you think, Jess?" and "What should I do?" routines. I hoped Mom's energy was still up, because mine was wearing down, and I just didn't know if I was going to be able to keep giving her what she needed to get through this one. Mostly I guessed it was that I was getting pretty involved myself these days. Oh, not the way Mom was, but in feeling good about myself. Enough to let me see that boys were stopping to talk to me and coming over at lunch to sit next to me. Most of them were nerds, but there was one cute guy in my math class, Victor, who started waiting for me when it was over and walked along down to my locker. He would hang around till I changed my books and then leave for his English class. I didn't know any of his friends and I often saw him talking to different girls, but never a special one.

That next day Victor was standing at my locker when school was over. "Did you understand that last problem?" he asked, and when I told him I did, he asked me to explain it to him. We walked outside and down the steps together, and I kept explaining and he kept frowning, trying hard to catch on. At the corner I stopped and took out the paper I was working on when the teacher broke it down; and when I showed it to him, his face suddenly lit up and he cried, "Oh, *now* I get it! It was that second step I kept doing wrong! Hey, thanks, Jessica."

He looked really nice when he smiled at me like that. He has a thin face, the sensitive kind that I like, and nice, warm brown eyes. His smile made the cold winter day start feeling awfully warm and cozy.

A group of kids crossed the street and began waving and calling to Victor. "Hey, we were looking for you!" one of the boys said. I didn't know any of them, but there were two pretty girls with those pearly smiles. Maybe Mom could teach me to do that. "Why don't you come down to The Place with us?"

"Yeah, maybe," he answered, then turned back to me. "Listen, thanks for explaining the problem. See you tomorrow."

"Sure. Bye." I walked on quickly, glad it had all happened so fast that I didn't have more than two seconds to think he was going to ask me something else. But the thing was, it didn't matter. All I could think of as I hurried home was that he had waited for me, had started to walk home with me. *It's a beginning*, I thought, my heart still racing. And then, when I saw Mom's car in the driveway and suddenly remembered about our appointment, I gave a prayer of thanks that Victor hadn't walked home with me, because knowing Mom he'd have been sure to find out we were going for a family therapy session. That's all I would have needed.

Dr. Gladstone was a woman. "A mother figure for Ben," Mom explained to me beforehand. "Dante and I agreed that would be best." At the time I almost said, "But he *has* a mother figure," but decided not to, because as I thought about it, let's face it, Mom might have been his mother, but she sure wasn't a mother figure. The funny thing was, Dr. Gladstone reminded me of Mom in certain ways, except that she was big and a little on the heavy side. But she was very warm and easy, in the sense that right after I met her I felt comfortable and as though I'd known her for a long time. That made me relax right away.

Her office was a room off the living room of her house, but it was more like a den than an office. There was a sofa and chairs and for a while there, it was like sitting around visiting with one of Mom's friends. I could see Ben liked her right off, too, and after we were all talking about general stuff for a while, I noticed she'd slip in little questions to one or the other of us, like, "Do you and Ben fight as much as most sisters and brothers?" to me; and to Ben, "How do you feel about your mother going to college?" We gave a lot of "I guess so" and "I don't know" answers at the beginning, but then she started asking Mom things like that: "Do you think your children have adjusted to your new way of life, since the divorce?"

Mom nodded. "I think they've done fantastically, better than I'd ever have thought."

"What about your new friends?" Dr. Gladstone asked her. "Have you been dating?"

"She sure has!" Ben piped up, and Dr. Gladstone smiled.

"Well," she asked him, "how do you feel about that, Ben?"

He shrugged. "It all depends. If they're nice guys I don't care. But when they're creeps like Randy—!" He shuddered, making one of his awful faces, and we all burst out laughing.

"So you don't like Randy," Dr. Gladstone prompted.

"*Didn't* like him," Ben corrected. "He's not in the picture any more. I took care of that."

Mom swiveled around to stare at him, but Dr. Gladstone just raised an eyebrow very slightly and said, "Oh? And how did you do that, Ben?"

Again he shrugged. "I ran away from home. Didn't you hear about that?"

"Yes, I heard something about it. But why don't you tell me. What did that have to do with Randy?"

"Well, things looked like they were getting pretty serious between him and Mom. The way they did with Daddy and Margie. Except I *like* Margie. But I couldn't see getting stuck with someone like Randy. So I—well, I got this idea. It was from a TV show I saw one day, about a girl who ran away from home when her parents said they were splitting up, because she figured that way they'd have to get together to find her and maybe then they'd start to like each other again. You know, all that junk about remembering all the good stuff they did together, and see what they did to their kid and each other, and all. . . ." He paused, and Dr. Gladstone said, "Yes? Well, how does that connect with Randy?"

"Oh, yeah," he went on, glancing sheepishly at Mom. "I figured that wasn't going to do me any good any more for Mom and Daddy, because that was all done and over with. But it hit me that it would work out my new problem, in a different kind of way." Mom and I looked at each other, then back at Ben, who was saying, "See, I figured this character just needed the littlest bit of pushing at and he'd fall away. You know, show his true, wimpy self. I thought if I ran away, Mom would fall back on him, to help her keep her courage up and all, and I knew he wasn't going to be able to make it. I just *knew* it. And I was right!" He turned to Mom and me. "Wasn't I?"

Mom spent the whole evening on the telephone in her room, with the door closed. The next morning she announced at breakfast: "We're not going to see Dr. Gladstone any more. Your father and I have decided it isn't necessary."

Ben laughed. "I could have told you that in the first place. She was pretty nice, though. Why does she have strangers come visit and tell her all their business? Is she lonely?"

Mom and I exchanged a smile. "No, Ben," Mom explained, "she's a person who's trained to help people solve their problems."

"But what are our problems?" he asked. "I still don't understand why we had to go to her."

"Neither do I," Mom said. "Now that I know. Anyway, it was well worth it."

"You mean we had to *pay* her?" Ben asked.

"Of course," Mom replied. "She's a professional."

"Oh, man, then I'm really glad we're finished. Who wants to pay out money just to sit around and talk about problems that you don't even have!"

Mom and I decided that was brilliant. The three of us left for school, and I hurried in the hope of getting a glimpse of Victor on my way to homeroom. When I met Elly at our usual place and told her the whole story, she kept slapping her head and saying, "I don't believe it! I don't believe it!" Then, after I finished, "I bet your mom must have kept you up half the night talking. Hey, what's happening with the new boyfriend?"

"Funny thing," I said, telling her about Mom being on the telephone. "I know she wasn't on the whole evening with my father. And then, strangest of all, she never came into my room to talk, just said good night and looked very closed-up." It was then I realized that that was the way she used to be when she was like a mother. And that morning, she had acted very cool and take-charge, more like Dr. Gladstone than Mom the cheerleader or Mom the activist. I didn't tell Elly all that; I had to wait and see if it kept up.

It did. A whole week of it, and Mom has become another different person. She hasn't come to me with a single problem, or even a question. I know she's been seeing Dr. Reynolds a lot, but she's hardly spoken of him at all, except to mention that they did this or that together, or that he told her this or that. She's still real cool about everything, and she seems more involved in what Ben and I do. In a way it's sort of a pain. The big tipoff was that the day after our visit to Dr. Gladstone, she started wearing skirts and pretty shoes, the way she used to. And today she wore her hair up.

She only has two classes today, and she's going to spend the rest of the day cleaning the house and cooking, because Dr. Reynolds—Dante—is coming to dinner. He sounds nice, and Ben and I are both curious to meet him.

Meanwhile, I have this other big problem now. Victor. He's been waiting for me at my locker every day after school and walking me halfway home. Even Elly says you can see he likes me. But he hasn't asked me out. I wonder if I ought to invite him over to listen to some albums or something. Elly says I should, but I'm scared. I thought about writing to Ann Landers. But now I'm just wondering if I should ask Mom instead. After all, she's gotten pretty experienced. I think her time has come to help me.